Loretta And The Drones

a novel by

John Ginsburg

Cover Art by Paul Bergman

Loretta And The Drones

ISBN 978-1-928149-30-9

Thank you
To Debbie Sayer for many helpful ideas.
To three derailed Winnipeg rockers, who argue almost
as well as they play: Dave, Dennis and Louis.

Chapters

1 The Disappearance of Loretta Selby

Winnipeg, November 7, 2017

To all appearances, it was an ordinary Tuesday evening at the Green home. Dishes had been done, lunches were made for school, the girls were happily occupied in their rooms down the hall. The girls - Kerry, 10 and Lisa, 8 - were mostly oblivious to any serious issues in their parents' adult world. That sturdy, dependable world had in fact been severely shaken by infidelity, and the past three weeks had been unspeakably difficult for their parents.

Jimmy and Karen Green had strongly concurred on the optimal short-term strategy, showing a familiar brave face and revealing nothing to the children. To the two girls, everything in their comfortable little world was exactly the same as it always had been. But their parents' reality was far different. Jimmy and Karen were reeling, living in a toxic fog, and struggling to communicate. Their predictable, harmonious relationship had been upended. It was a fearful time, not knowing where things were going or even how to talk about it. Conversations between the two were painfully awkward and limited to short, muffled extrusions, usually ending abruptly with a hurtful remark. When would they find the time to genuinely try and resolve things, to obtain some clarity? Or were they just avoiding it?

As Jimmy and Karen sat down to watch the 8 pm local news, their tense and difficult situation was about to receive a further sharp jolt. Jimmy sat in the old oak rocking chair, directly in front of the TV, remote in hand and a cup of tea

1

beside him. Karen sat to Jimmy's right, on the leather love-seat, reaching reflexively for her knitting as the news anchor introduced the lead story.

'Winnipeg police have issued an urgent appeal to the public for any information they might have about a missing Winnipeg woman, Loretta Selby, from the West Kildonan area of Winnipeg. Police spokesperson Ravinder Singh has asked anyone having any information regarding the woman's whereabouts to contact police immediately.'

It took a fraction of a second for Jimmy and Karen to fully register the woman's name. In that fraction of a second, as the video frame switched to the police press conference, Jimmy was on the point of making a derisive comment about the size of the policeman's blue turban, and how jobs like his never went to ordinary men any more. Karen was unhappily well-used to such remarks from her husband and she bristled in anticipation, hoping the two girls wouldn't hear their father. No matter how many times she called Jimmy on it, it didn't seem to make any difference. He could be such a jerk. But the missing woman's name hit them both at exactly the same time and Jimmy's words never came. Instead, he froze and the blood rushed from his face. He looked over at Karen, who was just as stunned.
'Loretta Selby?' said Jimmy, incredulous. 'It can't be.'
'Shush' said Karen. 'Let's listen.'

Standing at a small lectern, the police constable read out his statement:
"Anyone knowing anything about the current whereabouts of Loretta Selby, of 1888 Smithfield Avenue, is asked to please contact their local police detachment. Ms. Selby has not been seen or heard from in more than three

weeks. She is fifty-one years of age, five feet six inches in height, with long brown hair, and is thought to have been driving a white, 2011 Hyundai SUV. Her picture and other information are posted online..."

As the statement was read, a recent picture of Loretta Selby appeared on the monitor. There was absolutely no doubt about it. It was her. Loretta. With her straight brown hair tied back in a ponytail, as she often wore it, and wearing a denim jacket. There was a hint of a smile on her face. It was a very recent picture. It might have been taken at the band's last gig, Jimmy thought. Elliot was taking pictures of everybody with his iPhone.

A journalist present at the small news conference asked the obvious question. "Is this being treated as a criminal case? Are there any individuals under investigation at present?"

"That's all we have to say for now" said Constable Singh, who then stood up and walked off camera.

Jimmy switched the channel, then turned the television off.

On top of the tremendous shock, it was a supremely uncomfortable moment. It was exactly three weeks and one day since Jimmy had disclosed his long-running affair with Loretta. Karen had been totally in the dark.

Committed to the appearance of normalcy and calm, Jimmy and Karen sat in frozen silence for a moment, their thoughts and reactions inaccessible to one another. Karen was the first to speak, looking over at her husband and keeping her voice down. 'Do you know anything about this, Jimmy? I'm sure you know a lot more than you've been telling me. Have you been in contact with her? Do you know where she went?' Though she hadn't spoken very loudly, Karen was immediately aware of having lost her composure. She looked anxiously in the direction of the girls' rooms, relieved that they were still out of hearing range.

Jimmy, still stunned by the news of Loretta's disappearance, was feeling a sense of panic. He knew he had to remain calm and he had to answer Karen carefully and quietly. 'No. I don't' he said. 'I've had no contact with her at all. I meant what I said. It's over. I have no idea where she is.'

Ten days later, Duane Selby - Loretta's husband and the lead guitarist in Jimmy's band - was arrested in connection with her disappearance.

2 Loretta

October 4, 2017

At 8 pm, Loretta Selby was intently making her way up the stairs from the basement, with two freshly-ironed shirts and a pair of black pants slung over her arm. She had her long dark hair tied back in a ponytail and was wearing an old, faded, gray hoodie, with *Tom Petty Free Fallin 1990* in pale purple lettering on the front. The hoodie was a prized souvenir, from a concert in Calgary she'd attended with her sister. On hearing the sad news of Petty's death two days earlier, she had immediately retrieved the hoodie from a downstairs storage closet, and worn it ever since.

As Loretta turned the corner at the top of the stairs, walking up into the kitchen, she crossed paths with Duane. He had his navy blue jacket on, clearly about to leave the house. The two made eye contact very briefly. 'I'm going out. See you later' said Duane. 'I can see that, Duane' answered Loretta, coldly. At the hostile tone, Duane stopped and turned to look at Loretta. 'Why?' he said, his tone, by contrast, rather complacent. 'What's the problem?' Loretta had continued walking into the kitchen. She stopped and looked back at her husband of 31 years. 'The matter? Nothing's the fucking matter, Duane. If I hadn't run into you on the stairs, I wouldn't have even known you'd left the house. I live here too, you know. I mean, no one's expecting you to justify every minute of your life.' With that, she turned again and walked away, through the kitchen and into the living room.

Duane either had nothing more to add or didn't especially feel like talking to thin air. Loretta heard the back door close and then the roaring sound of Duane's black F-150 truck starting up. She didn't know where he was going. Maybe drinking with a few of his buddies. Or maybe he was going to buy something somewhere. Maybe he was fucking some other woman, having an affair like she was. She didn't know and she didn't really care a whole lot. But she certainly deserved to know if was going to be out. And at least to have some vague idea for how long. They still lived in the same house.

It wasn't all that different from the way it had been five years ago, she thought. Even ten years ago. What did it amount to? She cooked and cleaned the house. She did her sewing work. Sometimes they ate meals together, usually while they were watching TV. They went over to Duane's brother's place once in a while. And that was about it. They hardly ever talked anymore, about anything. If they did, it sounded fake. They hadn't had sex in years. He'd been sleeping in the second bedroom. She couldn't imagine ever kissing him or fucking him again. With or without Jimmy in her life.

The marriage was way past its best-before date. It was worse than watching paint dry. It was like watching the paint after it had dried, watching it fade into nothing. If it was supposed to be some kind of endurance test, she should get the gold medal, that was for sure.

At least he brought home a paycheque, she had to give him that, digging holes and filling them up again, day after day, same as he'd done for thirty years.

Maybe he was as numb to it as she was. Maybe it didn't matter to him anymore, like it didn't to her. Maybe he was just as worn down by the years. Or maybe he was actually content. As content as a guy like him could ever be. When he wasn't working at his job, he was working on his vehicles in the big workshop-garage in the back yard. It was like a used car lot out there. In addition to Loretta's

6

2011 Hyundai SUV and the Ford truck Duane drove, there were always one or two other vehicles in the driveway or inside the garage; some giant truck he'd bought from somebody on Kijiji, or some washed-up old Mercedes. He'd fix a vehicle up and drive it a little for a few months, and then he'd sell it over the internet to somebody else. Losing money as often as he made money. And then another one would show up a few days later. Or he'd decide to build something, or fix something around the house, like the bathroom in the basement, and the cedar shed in the back. And it would take years and still never get done. He always had to do everything himself and he always had to get the lowest price on materials.

And he had his band, The Drones. Well, that was a good thing for both of them; that's how she'd met Jimmy.

Jimmy. She was in love with him. And he was crazy about her. It had been well over a year now. They were like a couple of rabid dogs; they couldn't be together for more than two minutes and he'd have her jeans down and his face between her legs, and then he'd fuck her like a madman. She knew Jimmy loved her, even if he didn't say it. He said he still loved his wife. And he probably did. But it was really fear. He was scared of losing his safe, secure little world. He didn't even want to think about it, he'd say. You have to face it Jimmy, she'd tell him. You can't possibly be cheating on her like you have been, and keep slipping back home and pretending everything's the way it should be.

And his daughters... She knew how much they meant to him. All he ever said was he couldn't ever destroy their life or make them unhappy. He just couldn't. He wouldn't be able to live with himself if he ever did.

It wouldn't be like that, she'd tell Jimmy. Marriages break up all the time. How many people did he know who had married someone and was still with that person? People deal with it and move on, she'd say to Jimmy. You'd still be

7

their dad; you'd still have them as much as you could, be with them. I'd help you. It would just take some time for people to get used to things, settle in to a new life. It would be better for everyone. It would be real; honest. You wouldn't have to lie anymore. You wouldn't have to feel guilty anymore. We'd have a real relationship. We'd be so good together, Jimmy, she'd say. Jimmy would just get that distant look in his eyes when they talked about it; scared, put-off, pushed away.

Jimmy just needed a good push, that was all.

Loretta set down the shirts and pants on the kitchen table and walked into the living room. She sat down on the modular black leather sofa, one of Duane's proud IKEA purchases, and mindlessly flicked on the television. The news was on. Catalonia was the headlining story. There was Trudeau, firmly pledging his support for Spain. Funny how it was okay for Quebec to vote for independence, Loretta thought. So what was the deal, then? If you weren't French, you were out of luck? After muting the sound and surfing through a few channels, she turned the television off.

One of Duane's acoustic guitars was lying on the end of the sofa. His Martin. He'd been playing while she was working downstairs. How long ago had be bought that guitar? Twenty years ago, maybe? He wouldn't let anyone else touch that guitar at the time. He'd kept it hidden away when anyone came over. "You like that guitar more than you like me, Duane" she used to say to him. That was their big joke at the time. "You're a pretty close second, Loretta" he'd answer. "You just have to tune up every once in a while."

Those were the days when they still had jokes like that together. Long ago....

8

Loretta's thoughts wandered wearily over the same, sad terrain that they always did when she was in a funk. At least he'd never hit her. And they didn't argue all the time. Not like some people she knew about. And he wasn't a heavy drinker, either. She probably drank more than he did. Maybe if they'd had a kid. If they'd adopted a baby. Maybe it would have been different.

As Loretta invariably did when she thought about not having children - torturing herself with how that may have changed her life - she soon re-routed herself by thinking about her sister Cathy, in Calgary. Cathy had had so many problems with her son Brendan. How many times had that crazy kid totalled a car, or been caught with drugs, or quit his job... He'd always end up moving back home for a while and then Cathy and her husband would just buy him another car and throw money at him. And then it would happen all over again...

Thirty-one years of marriage. Maybe if they'd travelled somewhere it wouldn't have been so bad. So monotonous. Anywhere. But Duane just wouldn't travel; didn't want to and wouldn't. They'd gone to Las Vegas for their honeymoon and then back there five years later. And that was about it. All Duane had ever wanted to do for his holidays was drive a camper out to a lake in Manitoba or Northern Ontario. Park it and sit there. Play cards and drink beer. Maybe go fishing once in a while.

Jimmy would want to travel; he had travelled already, to places like Mexico and Jamaica. Duane would never go to places like that; even if you paid him.

She just didn't want to keep doing it anymore; keep living the same nothing life. With a guy she didn't want to be with. How could she? There was nothing to look forward to. There was nothing that made her happy anymore. Except for Jimmy.

She'd thought about leaving Duane a hundred times, maybe a thousand times. How she might do it; what she'd say to him. How she'd support herself, where she would live. How they would divide things up... money. How Duane would react. What would he do? Would he go crazy? Try and stop her? Come after her? Would he cooperate; give her what she deserved, or would he be a major asshole and try and cut her out of everything? Maybe he'd beg her to stay...

Or maybe Duane would just be relieved. Maybe there wouldn't be any kind of big reaction?

It was a typical evening for Loretta. Around and around in her head, she'd have the same thoughts, over and over again. And then she'd have a glass of wine or two. Try and forget about it for a while. Watch a little television. And then turn in for the night.

A whole lifetime they'd spent together. Come and gone. Their whole adult lives. But so what? So what? What did looking back ever do for you?

They'd met in high school. Loretta Barr, as she was known then, had grown up in the north end of Winnipeg, on Enniskillen Avenue, in a small, two-bedroom white stucco house, three houses from the corner of Enniskillen and McGregor Street. Her father was a roofer and her mother was a cleaning lady, which left Loretta under the youthful direction of her older sister Cathy a lot of the time. The two girls were very close and learned how to take care of themselves at a very early age.

As high school students, Loretta and her sister attended Garden City Collegiate on Jefferson Avenue, a few miles north of Duane Selby's school. Loretta was eighteen years old, in Grade 12, when she first met her future husband. The occasion was a Friday night dance at her school, in the fall of 1984, with Duane's band, The Detonators, providing

10

the music. The band played mostly seventies rock and roll songs, with a good measure of heavy metal. Duane had just turned seventeen. He was the rhythm guitar player and the only member of the band under eighteen. One singular feature of the band was a throwback to the sixties: dancers. Three shapely young women in skimpy dresses danced on pedestals on the stage. This was the bright idea of the band's twenty-year-old lead guitarist, whose girlfriend was one of the dancers.

Loretta was a highly confident young woman, and as strong-willed as she was direct. She was just as sexy as those dancers, she told her girlfriends that night, and she could dance better than all of them. Her friends laughed and dared her to offer her services to the band. At the band's first break, that's exactly what she did, breezing across the gym floor in her tight jeans and black boots, approaching the guitar player sitting off to one side. That turned out to be Duane Selby. She introduced herself, and, in the most flirtatious voice she could muster, asked him if the band was looking for another girl, assuring him that she was a better dancer than every one of the three they had, and that she had way sexier legs. The young Duane Selby was more than a little embarrassed by Loretta's brashness. He'd never heard any girl ever talk like that. And he thought she was so amazingly beautiful that he shouldn't even be looking at her. All he managed to blurt out in response was 'Um, I don't think they're looking for anybody else right now. I mean, *we're* not looking for anybody else right now. But...' 'Hey, no problem' said Loretta. 'Like I said, my name's Loretta Barr. Give me a call if you are. I could like, audition for you guys.'

Duane was totally knocked out by Loretta and certainly was not about to forget her name.

A tawdry career as a go-go dancer was not in the cards, however. Though opportunity almost knocked. Not long after that fall school dance, The Detonators lost two of their three dancers. First to go was the bass player's girlfriend. The jealous outbursts had become too much for her. What was she supposed to do? All the guys gawked at her and lusted for her at the side of the stage, wanting to talk to her at breaks. Well, of course they did. The boyfriend was making her miserable. So she broke up with him and quit. Next came the lead guitarist's girlfriend, who abruptly quit when she learned she was three months pregnant. Immediately, the one remaining dancer - not involved romantically with anyone in the band - insisted she should now become the middle dancer, the most prominent position. When no such commitment was offered, she quit too, leaving in a storm before any discussion about new dancers had even begun. Ground down by the negative volley, the three senior members of the band decided they should have no dancers at all for the immediate future.

Through all the band's high drama, Duane was constantly thinking of Loretta, hoping to get the chance to contact her. Because of his quick thinking, that chance materialized, even if it wasn't about Loretta dancing. With the indignant exit of the third dancer, the band also lost the services of her loyal sister, who had been looking after tickets and taking money at the door for their gigs. When the obvious need for a replacement was voiced, Duane had the perfect solution. He knew a girl who was super good in math, who was thoroughly honest and who was easy to get along with. In truth, he knew none of those things about Loretta, but it didn't matter. She was in; all Duane had to do was call her.

3 The Drones

October 5, 2017

It has often been said that choosing the name for a rock and roll band is one of the lowest of art forms. The vast majority of band-names are mocked soundly and then quickly disappear into the ether. But *The Drones* was a name that had enjoyed a measure of longevity in the city. Perhaps it was because people found the name easy to ignore. At any rate, as Nathan Rose, the progenitor, proudly told anyone who cared to listen, his brilliant idea for the name occurred in the early nineties, well before its entrenching in the western lexicon as an aeronautical and military term. Rose was the original drummer for the band, happily pounding his way through two inconspicuous years of basement practices and occasional gigs. To the bewilderment of his mates, Rose abruptly abandoned his career in rock and roll in 1997, becoming a rabbi in a small reform synagogue in the city's north end. And though the move was entirely of his own volition, Rose loved to claim he had suffered the same fate as Pete Best, gleefully adding that his first choice for the band's name had been The Beat Pests.

Following the band's inception in 1995, The Drones' lineup and status changed regularly. In present times, only the band's founder, Duane Selby, remained from those earliest days. Selby, now 50 years of age, was a talented lead guitar player, a difficult, aggressive man who relished his dominant role in the band. Virtually all the important decisions over the years had been Selby's, as he sustained the band through long periods of inactivity and change after change in personnel. As presently constituted, The Drones featured a keyboard as well as lead guitar, rhythm guitar, bass guitar and drums.

One thing had never changed about Duane's band: the kind of music that was played. It was an old-time rock and roll band, playing songs almost entirely from the nineteen sixties and seventies. A few of the songs were from the late fifties. They sounded, in 2017, just like the bands of those earlier times.

It was a chilly, fall evening. As was invariably the case, Duane was the first to arrive at the former strip-mall where the band currently practised. At 7pm, it was already starting to get dark. The drab-looking site was situated on Corydon Avenue near the CN tracks. It had once hosted a large grocery market and four other smaller shops. After sitting vacant for more than a year, the disregarded side-by-side units were still struggling to make a comeback. Recently, the largest unit had been leased to a government-funded day care centre. All of the remaining units were still available for sale or lease.

The band practised in what had most recently been a yoga studio. Entrance from the outside led into a long, narrow reception area, with a bathroom at one end and a door at the other end, which opened into a forty foot by twenty foot windowless room. A large storage closet had been left behind, situated at one corner of the room, and which the band made good use of. Folding metal chairs and a small office desk had been moved into the room from the reception area. Aside from a couple of wooden stools and the band's equipment, the only other furnishings in the room were a number of throw-away chairs brought by various members of the band. These were scattered randomly in the middle of the room: four old, discoloured

PVC patio chairs and a pair of unsightly rattan chairs, still usable but coming apart in places.

White Tama drums were set up along a wall adjacent to the closet. The keyboard, speakers and amplifiers formed a semi-circle around the drums, extending out onto the worn hardwood floor. Microphone stands, cords and metal chairs occupied the same positions they had at the end of the previous practice. Two cases of bottled water sat on the floor beside the amplifiers.

As a practice space, it was a very economical find by Duane: for a hundred and forty dollars a month, the band had twice-a-week access, with all the power they needed. Duane had neatly avoided any cost to himself with a simple dodge, informing the others that the rental was a hundred and seventy-five a month, to be split equally five ways. Why not, he thought? He'd found the place, made the contact and set it all up, hadn't he?

Wearing a faded black leather jacket, black jeans and worn, white trainers, Duane was carrying a guitar case in each hand. One was an old grey case with a faded pattern on it, scratched and scuffed by years of packing and moving equipment. Inside it was an old seventies Stratocaster, for which he claimed to have been offered fifteen thousand dollars. The other case was newer, plain black, and contained his ten-year-old Gibson Les Paul. Two additional guitars had to be transported from his car into the building, a much newer Stratocaster, as well as a Telecaster he'd recently purchased.

At a quick glance, aside from his flat, broad nose, Duane Selby had a rather unremarkable appearance. He was stocky, of slightly below-average height, with dull brown eyes and dull, greying, brown hair. But on closer inspection, his physical appearance more than hinted at his rough, aggressive nature. He had large, menacing biceps that he loved to display, usually wearing t-shirts with extra-short sleeves and muscle shirts in summer. This was not the result of conditioning or working out, but simply a direct product of his lifestyle, which included thirty years of hard physical work in the construction industry. Matching tattoos on both of his arms were gaudy relics from the nineteen-eighties, long before tattoos became competitive badges of honour for young people. Duane also carried a nasty, two-inch-long scar on his person, on the right side of his neck. While it was much faded by the passing years; it was still visible, the lasting mark of a drunken fight at the age of 18, in which Duane was slashed by a length of cable.

Anyone who knew Duane, knew to tread carefully around him and that there were times when you just had to keep your mouth shut. Not that he was difficult to be with all the time; he could be a lot of fun and knew how to have a good time. And he was generally a pretty loyal guy. But he had a mean, explosive temper and you certainly had to pick the right time if you wanted to press for something he didn't want.

As far as running the band went, it was Duane's show all the way. His way or the highway. He'd always ask what the others thought, but once he decided what he wanted, the conversation was over. You could argue with him, but if you did, you risked being cut down to size in no uncertain terms; maybe even having your ass kicked out of the band. Every new player that joined the band quickly learned how intimidating Duane could be and how best to maintain the band's dicey equilibrium. But the thing was, it was a *good band*. And mostly because Duane was such an incredible guitar player.

Within minutes of Duane's flicking on the lights, getting out his pedals and turning on his amplifier, the others began to show up. Second to arrive was Jimmy Green, the rhythm guitar player, wearing round, Ray-Ban sunglasses and carrying his guitar. Tall and lean, blue-eyed and soft-

16

spoken, Jimmy was the oldest member of the band, at 54 years of age. And he was easily the biggest throwback. He had long, straight, shaggy brown hair - starting to grey - and wide, flared sideburns to match. He always wore blue jeans and cowboy boots, regardless of the season and regardless of the occasion. Jimmy worked as a janitor for the St. James School Division, a job he'd held since his mid twenties.

'Hey Duane' said Jimmy, as he walked in. 'How's it going?'

Until recent weeks, Jimmy had been able to keep it all separate in his head, compartmentalized. When he was talking to Duane, or practising with him, or playing gigs, he wasn't really thinking about Loretta. Or at least he wasn't thinking about Loretta in relation to Duane. Or about Duane in relation to her. Duane was just the lead guitar player, one of the five guys in the band. Jimmy genuinely got into the music and just played. It was like being in another world. The fact that he was fucking Duane's wife, and had been for well over a year... well, that just got politely shoved to the back of the stage, out of sight. Mostly. Of course he thought about it *a little*; he was only human, after all. But it just didn't have anything to do with Duane or the band. Not really. It was just about him and Loretta. And when he was with Loretta, he never thought about Duane. Or about Karen. When he was with Loretta, it was just the two of them, for as long as they had, usually an hour or two. He just wanted her; he just wanted to feel her; to taste her; to fuck her. That's the way it had been; it had nothing to do with anyone else, nothing to do with the rest of his life.

And, until lately, his thoughts about Loretta had never got in the way of his home life, with his wife Karen and his kids. It was the same between Karen and him as it had been before he'd ever met Loretta. They did the same things, shared the same things, talked the same way together. They still made love once in a while. It was still good between them. Loretta hadn't changed that. When he did think about the situation, it was easy to explain to himself; easy to rationalize. And he just hadn't felt very guilty or troubled about it. He was as good a dad and as good a husband as he had been before Loretta. Lying about going out on Monday nights was a little lowdown, but that was about it. But how many couples tell the truth to each other all the time? Besides, it was kind of a reasonable lie. Kind of a good lie. He was supposed to be going out for guitar lessons every Monday night. That's what he'd told Karen. And he really *did* want to improve his playing. And he really *had* contacted the guy who gave lessons, even though he'd never gone.

With him and Loretta, it was just physical; it was just amazing sex. At least, that's what it *had* been. For Loretta too. That's what she'd said from the very beginning. That's what they'd both agreed. Neither of them was supposed to be blowing up their world. Karen and his kids were his life; his real life. He loved Karen. His life and his home with her and the kids meant everything.

Until lately, for the most part, things had been great. They'd both faithfully kept the bargain. There were the occasional times that Loretta had kind of lost it, and gotten very emotional. Then she'd start talking about wanting a *real* relationship, about her leaving Duane and him leaving Karen. At first, Jimmy had thought it was no big deal. It was just the great sex talking. And she was a woman, so what else should he have expected? Usually he had no trouble calming her down, saying enough to satisfy her. Then it was a clean escape, when she dropped him off. The next time they met, it would be the same as ever, like nothing had happened. That was the way things *had been*, until the last month or so. Now, Loretta was freaking out every time they met. Crying, getting upset... She kept telling him she wanted more. And she'd been pressuring him, threatening him. Especially the last two times they'd been together. Jimmy was trying to figure out how to deal with the situation. Something had to be done. It was weighing on him, worrying him.

So as Jimmy walked into the band's practice area, he was looking at Duane more anxiously than usual, and trying not to let it show. Duane is a scary dude, Jimmy thought, glancing over at him as he walked in. Mean. Jimmy had seen many times how Duane's temper would flare over almost nothing in the band. What if Duane found out about him and Loretta? He'd go frickin' psycho; there was no doubt about it. Would Loretta ever tell him? Jimmy asked himself the question for the thousandth time, trying hard to believe she wouldn't. Trying to convince himself. She had a lot to lose. And she *had to be* afraid of the guy. What would Duane's reaction to her be?

Duane looked over at Jimmy. He had just turned on the PA system. 'Jimmy' he said, by way of bland greeting, and then, referring to Jimmy's ever-present sunglasses, added with a derisive chuckle 'Jeez. Are those fuckin' things riveted to your head?'

Most of the time, Jimmy didn't react to Duane's little digs. Unless he felt like some kind of smartass answer. On this night, in his troubled state, he reacted more out of nervousness than anything else. 'Jealousy will get you nowhere, Duane' he said.

Duane ignored the comment and checked the volume of the mike he'd just turned on.

Composing himself, Jimmy took his cherished red Gibson 335 out of the case, turned on his amp and plugged in. After tuning his guitar, he tapped the microphone on the middle stand, where he always stood. 'Test. 1, 2, 3.'

19

Duane repeatedly played a short lick on his Stratocaster, trying one pedal after the other.

Jimmy had been with the band for two years, one of two people recruited to replace the previous rhythm player, Greg Mazur. Mazur had also been the lead vocalist for the band. He had left the band in a rage one night, in the middle of a practice, after a fiery confrontation with Duane over money. Since The Drones were committed to a pair of good-paying gigs a few weeks later, they had to scramble to find a new vocalist right away. Five potential replacements were quickly contacted and auditioned. The only good vocalist among them was Elliot Munroe. He didn't play guitar, but he did play some keyboard. After Elliot joined, Jimmy was added a month later.

Elliot was the next to show up, as the outside door again opened. He hesitated a moment, holding the door open, looking back toward the parking area, where drummer Norman Jones had just pulled in.

'Jeez, close the door, Elliot' said Jimmy. 'It's cold out there.'

'Hold on' answered Elliot, 'Jones is right behind me.'

The two men walked in and exchanged greetings with Duane and Jimmy.

Elliot Munroe was the youngest member of the band, a 45-year-old accountant, husband and father. Puffy-faced, with a pale complexion and thinning red-blonde hair, his conservative appearance and retiring manner belied the raw power of his singing voice and how intensely he got into rock and roll. On this day, as usual, he showed up at practice in his regular work attire, smartly dressed in a jacket and tie. One of Elliot's most conspicuous physical traits was the way he constantly adjusted his black, rectangular-framed glasses over his nose, never seeming to find the right position. What served him best in the band, besides his great voice, was his quiet, agreeable disposition.

Almost none of the band's petty conflicts ever really got to him. His tastes in music were broad and eclectic, ranging from The Tragically Hip to John Mayer to Jet to heavy metal. He liked to sing sixties songs too, and he especially liked to perform, so the band's frequent gigs suited him just fine.

Something else distinguished Elliot Munroe in The Drones. As the only person in the band with a university degree, he was the frequent subject of special treatment, mockingly accused of talking down to the others or thinking he was better than them. It was no different than every other band he'd been in. Usually he would just laugh off such comments; either that or cleverly play along with them.

Norman Jones - Jones, as everyone called him - took off his burgundy-coloured hoodie, dropped it on a chair and without further ado, stepped between the amplifiers and barged his way behind his white drums. He briefly fiddled with the hi-hat and then thumped the kick pedal a few times before reaching for a pair of sticks.

A tall, burly man, Jones had played in The Drones for more than ten years, longer than all of the others, except of course for Duane. He'd actually known Duane since the two were teenagers, when they'd both attended St. John's High School in West Kildonan. And while they had never been particularly good friends in high school, they had remained in touch and both still lived close to their childhood homes.

In his day job, Jones gamely plugged away at Canada Post, where he had enjoyed a long career as an inside worker. Like Duane, he had been married to the same woman for nearly thirty years. He and his wife Rae had first met when they were both 21 years of age. They had raised two sons, who were now in their twenties and living on their own in the city.

This was actually Jones's second tour of duty with Duane's band. He had been the band's second drummer, following the mercurial Nathan Rose. When the band became inactive for a number of months, Jones joined another group, so he was unavailable when Duane started up again. Not a particularly flashy drummer, Jones was steady and dependable, which suited Duane perfectly. Like many drummers, Jones was often a neutral sounding board for the competing and sometimes difficult personalities in the band. He was also the resident funny-man, inventing ridiculous alternatives to song lyrics and torturing the others with his silly jokes whenever he could.

The last member of the band to arrive, twenty-five minutes after everyone else, was the bass player, Dave Candon. One year younger than Duane, Candon was five-foot nine inches in height and slight. He was blue-eyed, with slicked-back brown hair and a thin, neatly groomed beard. He was from Flin Flon, in northern Manitoba, where he'd worked in the mine for nearly twenty years before moving to Winnipeg. After bouncing around for a while, he'd landed his present job in shipping and receiving at Costco. He was twice divorced and presently living on his own in a downtown high-rise. He'd been playing in rock and roll bands since his early teens. Duane had found him on Kijiji in 2010.

Known universally as Can or Cans, Dave Candon was one of those people who are perpetually late, no matter what the circumstances. By the time he sauntered through the door, wearing a black Winnipeg Jets touque, his waiting mates were thoroughly annoyed.

'Where the fuck *were* you, Cans?' said Jones, his tone perfectly expressing everyone's irritation.

None of them expected anything resembling a satisfactory answer to the question and they didn't get one.

'Hey guys, what's up?' answered Candon, expertly brushing off the question. 'You been missing me?' He took his Fender bass out of the case and plugged it into his amp.

Everyone in the band was well used to Candon and his seeming inability to ever be on time. It didn't matter how many times you reminded him or how much abuse he took when he was late; he just never showed up on time. But Duane loved his playing and especially how quickly he could identify chords and patterns, so his position in the band was pretty much secure. Another thing Cans had going for him, was his skill at shooting pool. Duane himself was a decent player and they had plenty of opportunities to play, at bars, legions and community clubs. It was a rare activity in which Duane had no need to dominate or dictate, which was a good thing, since Cans was virtually unbeatable. Aside from an array of impressive bank shots, and tricky combinations, Cans regaled the others with colourful stories of his teenage years, when he'd played on the warped floors of Freedman's legendary pool hall in Flin Flon, playing the Bear brothers, Johnny and Jimmy.

'Okay, let's get going' said Duane, impatiently. '*Johnny B Goode*.' He ripped into the unmistakeable intro and they were off.

Or they were *almost* off. Only a few seconds in, Duane stopped. They had just passed the part of the intro where there was a one-beat accent on the drums. Jones had done his thing, but Duane didn't like it. Duane wanted it *exactly* like the record, where the accent is just slightly off beat. Duane looked back at Jones and quietly said 'No. Let's try it again.'

For all five players, including Duane, this most recent edition of The Drones was the first band in which they had played any Chuck Berry songs. *Johnny B Goode* had been suggested by Dave Candon, one night when the band was discussing which Beatles songs they might add to their list. *Roll Over Beethoven* was mentioned, a Chuck Berry song, which led to Cans suggesting *Johnny B Goode*. It had been three months since they had first learned the song. Despite Duane's pickiness about the song, they all loved to play it. In any case, the song had joined a number of others near the bottom of their list, and it been a month since they'd last run through it.

No one was surprised that Duane was putting Jones through the mill. It had been the same almost every time they'd run through the song in the past. The only question was how many times Duane would want to repeat the intro. And how much time the two of them would waste arguing about it. When they'd first learned the song, Jones had pointlessly tried to defend himself: 'It was probably a mistake on the recording' he'd said to Duane. 'When was it, 1959 or something? It was probably accidental. They probably spliced part of the intro from another take, and it was just off a bit. Or maybe they didn't want to pay for more studio time to redo it. It sounds better right on the beat. Nobody will know the difference, anyway.' Duane was distinctly unmoved by Jones's reasoning. '*I'll* know the difference, Jones' he growled. 'I want to do this like the record. Let's try it again.' After a few more starts and stops that night, finally Duane was more or less satisfied with the drumming. 'Listen to the fuckin' songs at home, Jones' he had coldly advised his drummer.

On this night, as the other three waited to come in, Duane started the song a second time, and stopped again at the same place. 'No' he said again to Jones, in a somewhat less friendly tone. The third time, Jones seemed to hit it exactly the way Duane wanted it, but Duane stopped again and started again. The fourth time, Jones was again right on the mark and Duane stopped again. 'You gotta get this right, Jones' he said. 'Listen to the fuckin' record at home.'

The other three stood waiting and listening, exchanging quick, knowing glances, tensed and ready to come in whenever Duane decided to continue through the intro. It was on the fifth time. Jones hit it right and they ran through the song. Everybody, even Duane, was happy with it.

It was a recurring issue in The Drones, common to any cover band. How closely were they trying to copy the original recording of a song? Any of the five players, not just Duane, would pick his spots - particular parts of particular songs - insisting that it had to sound like the record. Or, just as strongly, taking the contrary position, that it didn't matter, that people should feel free to do it their own way, that it sounded better that way.

Johnny B Goode was one of those songs for Duane. It wasn't just the drumming in the intro. Elliot Munroe had been the man on the spot for the same song on a different occasion. That night, Duane wasn't happy with the end of the song, where there's a repeated back and forth between the lead guitar and the vocalist, where the vocalist sings "Johnny B Goode". Whether it was more a matter of Elliot's individual vocal style or Duane's pigheadedness, whether it was nitpickingly trivial or not, the rest of the band stood mutely by while the two of them repeated the offending part several times. Duane impatiently sang the part himself, in his gruff voice, to show Elliot how it should be done. By the time Duane was satisfied, Elliot was at the end of his rope, which was extremely unusual for him, as he almost never let anything faze him. At that point, Elliot turned off his microphone and reached for his jacket. 'Why don't you do the vocals on this one, Duane' he said quietly, and then left the practice. Next practice, nothing more was said about it.

If it was Duane who wanted a song a certain way, that's the way it was going to be. It was his band. People still argued with him, but it was almost always futile.

Conversations about how someone was playing something could start off constructively, but they could get hostile in a hurry. Especially if they didn't involve Duane directly. And they could be quite hurtful. But mostly, people rolled with the punches; they'd all played in bands for years so it was nothing new. Somehow the bruised egos survived. At least, most of the time.

As in any band, The Drones had established their own particular social structure and respected a sensible pecking order. Jones, as the one who had played with Duane the longest, felt the most comfortable dealing with Duane and often acted as a buffer between him and the rest of the band. Dave Candon, a pacifist at heart, was closely aligned with Jones, the two of them occupying the traditional positions of the bass player and drummer, at the bottom of the totem pole. If he ever had a problem with something, he filtered it through Jones. Elliot was Mr. Agreeable, calm and unruffled, getting on with everyone, rarely critical of anything and usually saying very little. Jimmy Green was Easy Rider, happy to be looking cool and playing in a good band. Being secretly involved with Loretta as he was, his direct dealings with Duane required equal measures of pragmatism and trepidation. Still, he had a lively mind and wasn't timid in expressing differences with the others or promoting his own preferences.

Duane, of course, was the undisputed alpha male, controlling and intimidating whenever he wanted to be. Whether he actually enjoyed being an asshole was unclear, but that's the way he was. Despite this, there was rarely any expression of mutiny, not even privately behind the scenes. He was simply accepted by the others. Not just because it was his band, but because he was such a talented guitar player. He would play solos by Jimi Hendrix or Eric Clapton or Joe Walsh that were note for note exactly like the record, perfect reproductions of the originals. At other times, he would freely improvise and it sounded even better. Everyone in the band loved it when he would stretch the solo parts to twice their customary length, as he often did. They just wanted to be part of it; he was that good.

With their next gig nine days away, at the Rockwood Legion on Wilton Street, the rest of the practice was a systematic run-through of the songs they intended to perform. Four recently added songs followed *Johnny B. Goode*: *Venus* by Shocking Blue, *Baby Please Don't Go* by Them, *Long Cool Woman in a Black Dress* by the Hollies and Del Shannon's *Runaway*. Then came the heart of their list, songs the band had been playing since its inception: Beatles, Stones, Animals and Yardbirds. With scarcely a break between numbers, the band flew gloriously through *I Saw Her Standing There*, *Twist and Shout*, *I Want To Hold Your Hand*, *Money*, *Nowhere Man*, *Eight Days A Week*, *You Can't Do That*, *You're Going To Lose That Girl*, *Satisfaction*, *Last Time*, *It's All Over Now*, *Honky Tonk Women*, *Jumpin' Jack Flash*, *Start Me Up*, *The House Of The Rising Sun*, *Bring It On Home To Me*, *Don't Let Me Be Misunderstood*, *We Gotta Get Out Of This Place*, *It's My Life*, *For Your Love*, *Heart Full Of Soul*, *I'm A Man*, and *Mister, You're a Better Man Than I.* Except for Jimmy or Jones forgetting to sing background in a few spots, and an occasional chord missed here or there, everyone was satisfied with these songs.

During their short break, Jones moved deliberately to entertain the others, as they sat on their tatty chairs, sipping from bottles of water. Elliot Munroe was the only smoker among them, and ordinarily he would have made a beeline for the door to go out for a cigarette. But he had only days earlier decided to try and quit, and so remained inside with the others. It was precisely because of Munroe's presence that Jones seized the moment, enjoying the maximum possible audience, casually launching into his latest joke, a Randy Bachman story. His fertile comedic mind had obviously been working diligently over the past few weeks, the bonus result of the band having added two BTO songs: *Taking Care Of Business* and *You Ain't Seen Nothing Yet.*

Anyone who knew Jones could usually see his lines coming a mile away. He often intended it that way. The previous week he had gamely contributed a bit of wordplay, which was met with mute disregard. "Hey guys" he'd announced enthusiastically, "Did you hear about that new Arabic musical that's breaking records on Broadway? It's a revival of an old American classic." He might as well have held up a sign which read Bad Punchline Coming. No one showed any interest whatsoever, so he simply forged ahead. "It's called *Yasser She's My Baby.*" A limp response from Jimmy was the only audience reaction: "How long did it take you to think of that one, Jones?" he said. "Or did you see that on the internet somewhere?"

But occasionally, Jones achieved true greatness, at least in his own mind. In this instance, both the detailed content and the inspired delivery showed that Jones considered the story a major achievement.

Speaking to no one in particular, Jones began: 'I was down at Long and McQuade, on Wall Street, picking up some sticks yesterday. Any of you guys know the guitar tec there, the guy with the big beard?' His tone was unhurried and matter-of-fact, sounding as if he was simply relaying a bit of mundane information. At first, only Jimmy Green was reasonably attentive, glad for the distraction. The others only half-listened.

They all knew the Long and McQuade store, and they all knew there were a number of guitar tecs there. Maybe one of them had a big beard...

'Anyway, I'm talking to this guy, asking him where to find something. And we start talking about bands. Larry something is the guy's name, I think. He was saying he doesn't play much anymore, and then we just started shootin' the shit. He said he knew Randy Bachman, going back to high school at Garden City Collegiate. I'm thinking, yah sure, you and everyone else in Winnipeg. There must have been 50,000 people in that class, I've heard that so many times.'

Now everyone was listening a little more closely, sensibly thinking that Jones was simply telling them how some guy had strung him along.

For his part, Jones knew he'd struck the right, matter-of-fact tone, and continued in exactly the same way. 'But then he started talking about his high school days and it sounded like he was kosher, like he really *was* in Bachman's class. He told me something I never heard before - how Bachman came up with the song *Taking Care Of Business*.'

'All the girls in their class had to do home-economics in those days. The boys did shop and automotive. There was this girl in the class named Terra Chiznick. She hated cooking and sewing and shit like that, and she was kind of a rebel. She just refused to do it sometimes. Maybe she wanted to do shop with the boys. Anyway, the girls had this class project. They had to bake a cake and ice it. And then everyone got to eat a piece and take some home. They were in groups of three or four. This Terra girl just refused to do it.'

Everyone in the band was well familiar with Jones and his antics. His stories and one-liners were usually nakedly telegraphed to the others; otherwise, any semi-coherent conversation he might broach was instantly regarded with suspicion. In this case, a rare achievement, no one in the room had any idea Jones was up to something. If he was, why would he be talking about girls baking cakes in home economics class?

'By that time, the other girls had kinda had enough of this Terra chick. She'd been pulling the same shit all year, getting out of doing the work that they all had to do. So they decided to get even with her. At the end of the period that day, when they'd finished icing the cakes, the teacher announced that everyone could cut themselves a piece of cake and then clean up. Terra didn't want any cake and refused to help clean up. Two girls distracted her, pretending to try and change her mind. Another girl sneaked up behind her with a whole cake, covered thick with icing, and absolutely plastered her in the face.'

For an instant, Jones paused dramatically, observing the somewhat puzzled faces and knowing his audience was still in the dark. Then he concluded the story, in the same factual tone.

'That's where the name came from.'

No one was quite sure what he was getting at and no one responded.

'The song' said Jones. 'The name of the song.'

'What the fuck are you talking about, Jones?' asked Duane finally, taking the bait on behalf of everybody.

'Well, think about it. What were they doing? They were caking Terra Chiznick.'

After delivering this line, Jones immediately repeated the last phrase in song, singing it to the tune of the chorus in *Taking Care Of Business.*

'They were caking Terra Chiznick, every day, caking Terra Chiznick...'

Too late, everyone realized they'd been completely had. Jones' triumph was complete.

'You're something else, Jones' said Jimmy, acting annoyed, though thinking he had to hand it to Jones on that one.

'Hey, I don't get it' said Dave Candon in mock ignorance, trying to ruin at least part of Jones' fun.

Duane had heard Jones tell his stories for so many years, that he mostly tuned them out, although he'd bought into this one. With a resigned shake of his head, he stood up, tightened the cap on his bottle of water and headed back over to his guitar.

Only Elliot Munroe chuckled a little, adjusting his glasses as he did so.

'I think we should sing that as the actual chorus' added Jones. 'See if anyone notices.'

As much time as they spent together, talking easily about almost anything under the sun - music, cars, sex, hockey, food, politics, money - the five members of The Drones communicated, proportionately, very little about their personal lives. This had nothing to do with any sort of personal inhibitions. Nor was it because they all had dark secrets to conceal, like Jimmy Green. It was more like an unspoken rule: as much as possible, real life was not to intrude on their magical rock and roll world, as if somehow it might be punctured or brought down to the ground. Any genuine exchanges bearing on family life or work or children - as infrequent as they were - typically occurred between two people at a time. Personal information was revealed in small, brief drips.

A good example was Elliot Munroe, the powerfully-voiced lead vocalist and keyboard player. Elliot had been in the band for over two years, but until recently, no one in the band knew either his wife's name or his son's name. Or anything else substantial about his circumstances. He lived somewhere in Fort Garry, that's about all he'd ever told anyone. All of them had heard him mention a wife a few times, as well as a son, but it was only in passing. Then, out of the blue one night, as he and Jones were shooting the shit, talking about American politics, Elliot mentioned that Shirley was kind of religious, that she wanted the kids to go to church on Sundays. 'Shirley. Your wife?' answered Jones. In short order, the information bled through to the other three: Shirley was the name of Elliot's wife and he had more than one kid.

Perhaps motivated by the Terra Chiznick story, Elliot again chose to communicate about his family on this night. This time it was Jimmy Green who found himself the provisional confidant, sitting next to Elliot.

'So, are you having a big turkey dinner for Thanksgiving?' Elliot quietly asked Jimmy.

A chill of realization hit Jimmy in a quick flash. Thanksgiving, he thought. Fuck. It was this coming weekend. He'd forgotten to talk to Loretta about it. Were they still on for Monday? He had to assume they were. Karen knew that his Monday night guitar lesson was still on. Although he wasn't going to it, of course; he never did.

'Um, yah' said Jimmy, in answer to Elliot's question. 'On Sunday. My wife's sister and her family are going to be over, and her mother. How about - '

'Do you do any of the cooking?' asked Elliot.

'That'll be the day. About all I ever cook is scrambled eggs or burgers on the barbecue.'

'So your wife does everything?'

'Mostly. I'll set the table, cut the bread, that kind of thing. Do the dishes... How about you, Elliot? You havin' a big family dinner?'

'We're having my mom and dad over. Shirley's parents are in B.C. But it kind of got messed up a bit. All three of my kids are supposed to be there, but it's not going to happen. We've been working on it for months.'

'Oh.'

'I can't remember the last time all three of them were together in the same place at the same time. I think it's only happened once or twice. It drives my mother crazy. She's the grandmother, so she wants to have all her grandchildren together. They all have different mothers, so it's World War Three any time you try to arrange something.'

'Wow. That must be tricky. What are the custody arrangements?'

'Todd lives with us. He's the oldest; 15. His mother is kind of out of the scene, but she still shows up once in a while. I have split custody with the other two. I'm supposed to have Devin 50/50 but his mom lives out in Anola so that doesn't always go so smoothly. She's got two other kids with the guy she's with; one of them's just a baby. Sometimes her car isn't running or she just doesn't feel like coming into the city. Plus, I've been at the top of her shit list since we split up.'

'Devin's the middle one?'

'He's the youngest. He's nine. Hayley is the middle one. She's thirteen, in grade eight. Her mom's in the city. We have her Wednesday nights for dinner and every second weekend. Holidays are always a problem, because Myrna thinks Hayley should be with her for every holiday, except the long weekends in summer. That's been the hardest one; Hayley. We've gone to counselling, court, all that nice stuff.'

'Myrna's her mom?'

'Yah. We had it all set up for this weekend. Then she changed her mind, a week and a half ago. And now Devin's mom is backing out too. It's like "You had her last Christmas" and "I'm sorry, but both Brad's parents and my parents are going to be at our place. They're getting older, especially Brad's parents." Bullshit like that.'

Stunned by Elliot's unexpected outpouring of personal information, Jimmy had no idea how to respond. 'Wow' he said. 'Complicated.'

'My mother goes nuts. She's talked to both of them on the phone, trying to change their minds. And then she gets on me to try and change their minds. We've been working on it for about two months. It's like a sit-com in our house.'

Just then, an empathetic response occurred to Jimmy, for which he instantly felt rather proud of himself. 'Your wife must be a very understanding woman.'

'Tell me about it. And now *she's* pregnant.'

'Shirley?'

The extraordinary little chat ended when the call came out from Duane. 'Let's get going, guys.'

Jimmy and Elliot joined the others.

'Okay' said Duane, glancing at a printed sheet of paper. 'Let's run through our second set for the fourteenth. Let's start with The Kinks. We're doing the two songs back to back, remember, as a medley. Jones bridges them on the drums.'

'Which one is first?' asked Cans. *'You Really Got Me?'* They're so similar it's hard to keep them straight.'

'All Day And All Of The Night' answered Duane. With that, he tore into the short intro, and after Jones' rim shot, the rest of the band followed.

The practice proceeded briskly and uneventfully, as they ran through songs by The Dave Clark Five, Cream, Them and a four-song Creedence Clearwater Revival medley. Then came a handful of slower songs, including *Red House* and *Hey Joe* by Jimi Hendrix and *Wonderful Tonight* by Eric Clapton. They were all songs that the band had been playing for some time and, in each case, a single run-through was sufficient. The songs sounded as good as they were ever going to.

Duane picked up the list again and quickly looked it over. 'We forgot one of the new ones' he said. '*Make Me Do Anything You Want.*'

'By Athlete's Foot In Mould Water' quipped Jones. 'Nobody remembers the name of the band that recorded this song. You know what we should do at the gig? Have a contest. The first person to name the band wins a prize.'

Duane decided to play along with Jones. 'And what's the prize, Jones?' he said.

'I don't know' said Jones, thinking in earnest. 'We could give out a baseball cap that says The Drones on it. It would be good advertising.'

'Except we don't have any baseball caps like that, Jones' countered Duane.

'Mere details, my friends' said Jones, smiling. 'Mere details. Or how about, they get to go out on a date with one of the guys in the band. They get to choose.'

Elliot decided to weigh in. 'Yah right, Jones' he said. 'Your wife would be real happy about that one.'

'Hey, it's band business, man' said Jones, thoroughly enjoying himself. 'My wife hardly pays any attention to us anymore. If I told her we got invited down to City Hall to play for Skippy Bowman, she'd just go "Whatever". Plus, you're missing a very important point, Elliot. It would probably be a guy that won the contest.'

'Let's do the song and call it a night' said Duane, swapping his Stratocaster for his Gibson.

Make Me Do Anything You Want had been suggested months earlier by Dave Candon, but the band had first played it only two weeks ago. According to the band's working rules, anyone could propose adding a new song. But everyone had to endorse it. In practice, this really meant that Duane had to support the idea. After that, the

35

song was added to the bottom of the band's wish list. Every second week, they rehearsed the top song on that list. If they all liked the way it sounded, they kept the song and added it to their permanent list. *Make Me Do Anything You Want* was one of the rare suggestions that was so enthusiastically embraced, it was immediately added to the permanent list, even before they'd tried it.

The song was one of a handful on which Jimmy Green sang the lead vocal. It was also a song in which Duane had decided to play the solo part exactly like the record.

'It's in G, right?' said Elliot.

'D' said Duane.

'Oh yah' said Elliot. 'It has that funny D.' He played the first few chords for himself.

Jones counted them in. 'One, two, three, four.' Duane and Elliot played the D and Jimmy came in: 'In the mornin' light...'

When they reached the solo in the middle of the song, Duane stumbled on a note and abruptly stopped, waving his hands. 'Let's do it again' he said. The second time through, Duane slipped again, this time at an earlier spot. 'Fuck' he said, annoyed. 'I can hardly hear what I'm playing. Are we too loud? Let's do it again.' The third time, the solo broke down at the same place it had the first time. They stopped again. This time, Duane was angry. 'I can't even hear what I'm playing' he said. 'How the fuck am I supposed to play when I can't even hear myself. We're too fucking loud. Elliot, Jimmy, maybe you guys should take off some of your volume.'

'We're playing at the same volume we have been all night' said Jimmy. 'Exactly the same mix. How does it sound to you, Jones?'

Jones said nothing in direct response to Jimmy, but offered a suggestion. 'Why don't you turn your amp in a little, Duane, toward yourself?'

'We're too fucking loud' Duane repeated, angry and insistent.

While the volume mix might have been a bogus issue, Duane's exasperation was certainly not. As hard as he could be on others' playing, he was hardest on himself. If he decided to play a solo exactly like the record, it had to be perfect. If it wasn't, his quick temper was sure to erupt.

Elliot and Jimmy turned down and they began the song again. Jones played as quietly as he could. This time, Duane tripped up right at the beginning of the solo. He was spitting mad. 'We're still too fucking loud' he said. 'I can't fucking hear myself.'

Elliot Munroe judiciously intervened. 'Let's call it a night; leave this one till next time' he said. 'It's late. We're all getting tired.'

4 Musical People

Jimmy Green wasn't the first man to have an affair with Loretta Selby. That dubious distinction belonged to a man named Ian Cooper, who had preceded Jimmy into the breach by a year. Cooper was ten years younger than Loretta; a gentle, sensitive man, with soft brown eyes. He was tall and good-looking, with a toned, athletic body. As Loretta put it to her sister Cathy, he was "one hundred percent gorgeous". To Loretta, what was even more attractive about him, when they first met, was how vulnerable he seemed, and how needy, having recently incurred deep wounds in the ways of love.

Like Jimmy, Cooper was a guitar player, and Loretta had met him in connection with Duane's band. But unlike Jimmy, he had never played with Duane. When Loretta met Cooper, he was in another rock and roll band, called Wally and the Winnipegs. The occasion was a four-band benefit concert, in support of Winnipeg Harvest, a community-based food distribution organization. At the Convention Centre that summer night, Cooper's band was up second and Duane's was last. Loretta was there too, spending most of the night in the company of the various musicians and their partners. Cooper was there on his own, having recently split up with his girlfriend. He and Loretta met, talked over a few drinks, and the flame was lit.

As affairs go, Loretta's affair with Ian Cooper was disappointingly short on passion, but long on problems. From the very start, Cooper was plagued by serious doubts, vacillating between making it with Loretta and wanting his old girlfriend back. After a few ambiguous months, dimly coloured by sporadic sex, Cooper's girlfriend moved back in with him. Loretta and Cooper broke off. But things didn't go well with Cooper and his girlfriend, and she moved out again. At least that's what Cooper told Loretta, who was fairly easily persuaded to start up with him again. He was actually seeing both women at the same time, and lying to them both. Eventually Loretta found out and dropped him cold.

Loretta had been appropriately careful in keeping her affair with Ian Cooper secret, creating timely excuses and covering her tracks whenever necessary. It hadn't been all that difficult. Because of Cooper's existential guilt and uncertainty, their actual trysts were infrequent. Over the course of a year, Cooper came and went from Loretta's life and Duane knew nothing about it. The only person she told about the affair was her sister Cathy.

With Jimmy Green, things were much different. They met every Monday evening, in a frenzy of lust and fucking. He could hardly wait to see her again. Maintaining secrecy required constant discipline and a much higher degree of caution.

As far as both Jimmy and Loretta were aware, no one knew about their affair. They had been meticulous in their deceit. Neither had said a word to anyone in their lives about it. And they followed strict rules. No phone calls, no texts, no emails. They met at the same safe place every time. If one of them didn't show, it was simply off for that night and they met the following week. That had only happened a few times.

But in recent months, things had fundamentally changed. Loretta was still careful and secretive, but she had fallen in love with Jimmy. She wanted a real relationship with him, not just hot fucking and snatches of conversation for a couple of hours every week. Many times she'd thought of telling Duane about the affair - as a way of forcing things to happen - but she was uncertain as to what she would say and she feared the consequences. It was all so complicated and unpredictable. Plus, it wasn't fair to do anything like that without Jimmy being in on it. Often she wished Duane would just find out on his own and take it right out of her hands.

Unknown to both Loretta and Jimmy, the veil of secrecy was about to lift on October 9, when they met as usual. It was a rather unlikely observer, Greg Mazur, who was in the right place at the right time, to whom the affair was revealed. Mazur was the former lead vocalist in The Drones, whose abrupt and angry departure had led to Jimmy Green and Elliot Munroe joining the band.

Greg had spent three stormy years with the band, years marked by recurring conflicts and unresolved hostility between him and Duane. Whether triggered by Duane's humiliating criticisms of someone's playing, his continuing dictatorial role in directing the band's affairs, or by simple differences over song selections, their arguments brought out the hardness and stubbornness in both of them. The two men had strong, clashing egos, and this ultimately destroyed their relationship in the band.

To Greg Mazur, music had long been a form of salvation. He had been performing ever since he was a child, when he would enthusiastically accompany his dad at family parties, singing country songs to the rapt applause of the guests. But any happiness and security he knew at home was cut short. His father abandoned Greg and his mother when Greg was thirteen. It was a heavy blow that neither he nor his mother ever really recovered from. Greg dropped out of school in Grade 10, leaving home and blaming his mother for the dark turn his life had taken. He lived with an uncle for a while, then with some older friends who had their own place. His mom was on social assistance for the rest of her life.

For a period of years, Greg gamely tried to make a living as a musician, but things never really clicked for him. He was in one band and then another, sometimes for a few years, sometimes only for a few months. Eventually, playing in a band became a part-time thing, practicing once or twice a week, playing a couple of gigs a month - as he did in The Drones.

Today, at 40 years of age, Greg lived in two worlds. There was his joyful and satisfying musical life; the intoxicating freedom of performing and the shared comfort of being in a band. On stage, in the band, he was an impressive, inspiring sight, with his raw good looks, his long hair tied back, wearing a black t-shirt and black boots, totally absorbed by the music. And then there was the rest of his life; a series of indifferent jobs, never enough money, living in one low-rent apartment after another; a constant struggle to get by. In recent years, he'd worked on and off as a house painter, taking whatever jobs came his way. But that work had mostly dried up, as younger people and immigrants did the same work for less pay. He also did residential yard work and snow clearing, but finding regular clients wasn't easy. His main source of income nowadays was driving a cab, vapidly steering his way out to the airport again and again, scratching out as many fares as he could. But in an overpopulated and highly protective industry, his income languished near the bottom. It was a dull, disheartening existence. He'd never been married, but he'd had a few close calls; a few lucky escapes. Mostly he'd bounced around from one relationship to another, from one beautiful face to another, from needy, lost souls to two-timing, manipulative women he barely got to know.

Life just hadn't been very kind to Greg Mazur. But he'd survived in one piece, more or less, and he didn't blame

41

anyone any more. He had learned to be resilient. His experiences had toughened him; hardened him. And he could still sing. He was never out of a band for long. Within weeks of leaving Duane's band, he was back in the saddle, lead vocalist for a five-piece band called Soul Doubt. The band played a lot of R and B and, most unusually, featured a talented and attractive female lead guitarist. Her name was Ricki Clark and it didn't take long for her and Greg to get romantically involved, with Greg spending most nights at her side-by-side in Southdale.

As far as vocalists were concerned, The Drones had been extremely fortunate in landing Elliot Munroe as a replacement for Greg Mazur. Elliot had the kind of strong, unique voice that people were instantly drawn to. The role of front man suited him well, too; he enjoyed introducing the songs and chatting with the audience, happily perched behind his keyboard, constantly adjusting his glasses and the position of his microphone. Even better, he always came to gigs and practices well-prepared, despite a demanding day job and an often chaotic domestic life.

But as good a vocalist as Elliot was, and as well-liked as he was, it was hard to argue that the band sounded as good as it had with Greg Mazur. Greg's voice was younger and more pliable than Elliot's, as well-suited to soft, romantic songs as to Motown or the Stones. While Elliot may have had a stronger voice, Greg could better emulate other vocalists. When Greg sang Stones songs, he sounded like Mick Jagger. When he sang *Eight Days A Week*, it was as close to John Lennon as he could possibly get. Not only that, but the band had *looked better* with Greg. Greg was tall and thin, five years younger than Elliot, and much better-looking. And with his long hair and hip clothes, he much more fit the picture of a rocker than Elliot.

Greg's final confrontation with Duane had been over money. They had hassled over money before, most recently about buying a new PA system. Greg didn't think they really needed one that badly. And he definitely didn't want to have to chip in to buy it. 'It doesn't matter what we say or what we want' Greg said to Duane on that earlier occasion, at practice, steaming mad. 'You just decide what you want to decide. What's the fucking point of asking anybody for input, Duane? It's bullshit. You just do what you want anyway.'

'Fuck you, Mazur' answered Duane with a scowl, as dismissive as he was angry. 'You've got a big mouth. But nothing ever came out of it that's any better or any smarter than anything I've ever said.'

Somehow, the band had survived that exchange intact, with Norm Jones and Dave Candon anxiously looking on in silence, hoping the two men would call it quits before coming to blows. But the next argument, a month later, spelled the end. It was a pleasant summer night, a Thursday. The band had gathered at the Regent Avenue Community Centre in Transcona, where they practised at that time. They had enjoyed a good-paying gig a week and a half earlier, a wedding social in Anola, a few miles out of the city.

With The Drones' well-earned reputation for performing at weddings, socials and other parties, gigs had been coming their way fairly regularly over that summer season, three or four times a month. The band was registered with the relevant local agencies, and the lion's share of their bookings came either through these agencies or directly from venue managers. Whenever an agency booked them, a percentage of their quoted fee was deducted by the agency before they were paid. Sometimes this percentage was negotiable, sometimes not. It was usually around ten percent. The balance was paid to Duane, who then split it among the band members.

Though he'd kept it to himself, Greg suspected that Duane had stiffed the other band members on a few occasions in the past. He had no concrete proof; the financial arrangements were always kept private between Duane and the client or agent. Greg had no idea if the others shared his suspicions. His feeling was that Jones and Candon were quite prepared to swallow whole whatever Duane dealt, believing they had no real choice in the matter.

It wasn't just a matter of fairness; Greg's radar was up for more practical reasons. Money was extremely tight in his personal life at that time; he counted on the cash coming in from gigs to get by.

And then, one day, Greg's suspicions were confirmed, in connection with the band's July wedding social in Anola. That gig had come about because of an old high school friend of Greg's, who had happened to see The Drones perform several months earlier. When the two renewed their acquaintance that night, the friend told Greg his sister was getting married. 'Hey, is she having a social?' said Greg. The seed was planted and The Drones got the call. Greg's friend had looked up the band's website and called the contact number, negotiating the deal with Duane.

A few days after that gig, Duane presented each of the other members of the band with an envelope, containing the tidy sum of three hundred and fifty dollars.

Greg was well aware that their band received varying amounts for performing at socials, especially wedding socials. In the past year, their fees had ranged from eight hundred dollars to eighteen hundred dollars. Still, fourteen hundred seemed a bit on the low side this time around. Greg knew that the bride's family was pretty well off; they would probably have accepted whatever price Duane had quoted.

If Duane was pulling something, there was an easy way to find out. Greg called the friend and asked him what the family had paid, devising a simple pretext for the question. Greg said he wanted to be sure Duane had passed along a special discount to the family, being that Greg knew them personally. The friend wasn't sure about the discount, he told Greg, but they'd agreed on an amount of eighteen hundred dollars with Duane. Did that include the discount? Yes it did, Greg told the friend, informing him that The Drones usually charged two thousand for wedding socials.

Greg did the arithmetic. Each of them should have been paid a share of four hundred and fifty dollars, not three hundred and fifty. Duane had skimmed four hundred off the top for himself. The gig was worth seven hundred and fifty bucks to Duane and three hundred and fifty to everyone else. He had Duane dead to rights.

Ready to confront Duane at the next practice, Greg deliberately arrived later than usual. He was nervous and waited in the parking lot for another several minutes until Cans showed up. Finally he did and the two walked in together. As they approached the small stage where the equipment was set up, Jones stopped playing, looked up and said hello. He'd been keeping time for Duane's guitar, as Duane played the solo part for *Red House* at low volume. Seated on a stool, Duane nodded as the two men walked up, continuing to play. Cans took a step up onto the low stage and took his guitar out of the case. As he did, Greg walked up just to the front of the stage and stood directly in front of Duane.

It was obvious to the others that Greg had something going on; he'd arrived late, with no guitar in hand, and his body language, as he stood in front of Duane, spoke for itself.

'Duane, I want to ask you something' Greg began, trying to remain as calm as he could. He'd rehearsed what he wanted to say. For the past few days, imaginary conversations had been going on over and over again in his head, keeping him awake in bed at night. In light of what he was going to say, he had little doubt that this would be the end of his time in the band. But that's how it had to be; he'd had enough of Duane and his dealings.

As soon as Greg spoke, Duane stopped playing and relaxed his hands, leaving them in position on the guitar. Looking up at Greg, he said 'Yah? What's on your mind?' instantly gearing himself up for whatever was coming. Without a sound, Jones laid his drumsticks on top of his floor tom-tom, folded his arms and looked on. Cans remained standing, frozen in place, realizing there was little point plugging in his bass.

'Can you explain to me how you divide up the money from gigs?' Greg's tone was unmistakably belligerent. The look on his face was grim and challenging.

After a short, ominous laugh, Duane answered. 'What's your problem? You know how it works.'

'Why don't you remind me? Just in case there's something I'm missing.'

'There's nothing to miss. Whatever we get from gigs is divided into four equal shares.'

'What about agency fees?'

'What the fuck are you getting at, Mazur? If there's a booking fee or an agency fee, that comes off first. You know that.'

'What if there's no agency fee?'

Duane was pretty sure he knew where Greg was going with his questions. 'Say what you want to say.'

'Like the Anola gig. The wedding social. There was no agency involved.'

'Maybe there wasn't. So what?'

'There's no "maybe" about it, Duane. I know the guy that contacted you for that gig. There was no agent. He called you directly.'

'What, are you tracking my fucking calls?'

In a twisted way, Greg was almost enjoying himself. He wanted to make Duane as uncomfortable as he could in front of the other two guys. Make him squirm like a snake. 'That's what happened, isn't it?'

Duane was visibly pissed off. He stood up, unstrapped his guitar, and placed it on a stand a few steps behind him. Then he looked back at Greg and answered him with a snarl. 'You saying I don't know what I'm doing? I don't know how to book gigs? Or maybe I just don't know how to count, ay? Maybe I'm not smart enough.'

Greg was confident and unflinching. 'I'm saying you stiffed us. You didn't give us what we deserved, Duane.'

Duane glared at Greg, his anger building. 'Fuck you, Mazur. I should re-arrange your fucking face for saying that.'

Jones knew Duane well enough to know that he meant business. He figured he'd try and cool things down a little, while he still could. He got up from his drums and walked around them toward the front of the stage, standing a few feet to Duane's left. 'Come on, guys' he said, looking at Greg and Duane in turn. 'Let's take it easy, take it down a notch. We're friends here. We're a band. Let's -'

Greg interrupted Jones, looking straight at Duane, maintaining the same cold, quiet tone. 'It's true. You got eighteen hundred for that gig. And we each got three hundred and fifty. There was no agency involved. Eighteen hundred divided by four is four hundred and fifty, Duane. You owe each of us another hundred bucks from that gig.'

Duane's fists were clenched; his whole body was tensed. He started to take a step towards Greg, but Jones was ready and quickly stepped in front of Duane, facing him and

extending his arms. 'Hold on, Duane' he said. 'Hold on.'
Duane partially backed off for the moment. Jones half-
turned his body, keeping his arm and hand extended toward
Duane as a gesture of restraint. 'Hey guys' Jones said, again
looking at the men in turn. 'Come on. Let's be civilized
about this. Everybody can say what they want to say. Let's
talk this out.'

Jones was broad-shouldered and tall, almost a head taller
than Duane. Standing on the stage in front of Duane, his
large body presented a considerable barrier between the
two men. Frustrated, Duane took a step to his right, his
body still tensed, glaring around Jones at Greg. Jones still
had his arms out. 'Get out of my fucking way, Jones' said
Duane, angrily. Then he directed a torrent of vicious
sarcasm at Greg. 'You think I don't know how to run this
band, Mazur? Ay? A hunkie like me can't add two and two,
right? Yah. What we really need is a fucking genius like
you to run things, don't we. Yah, you got everything
figured out, don't you Mazur. Like the accountant I just had
to pay for doing the tax return. And the annual bill for the
website. Oh! Pardon me. Isn't it too bad these things
actually cost money. I guess we should have left those
things up to you.'

'That's bullshit, Duane. That's the first time I've ever
heard you mention an accountant since I've been here. And
you can get a website for peanuts.'

'Fuck you, Mazur. You know where the door is. Why
don't you go and start your own fucking band?'

Greg stood his ground. 'Maybe I will, Duane. But I want
the hundred bucks you cheated me out of.'

Jones could see that the situation was at the breaking
point. Turning to face Duane, he took a step to his left,
again putting himself directly in front of Duane, and again
holding out his hands as a barrier. Duane brought his right

48

hand up to Jones' side, giving him a firm push to the left. But Jones resisted and stayed where he was.

'Come on, Duane' said Greg, egging Duane on, daring him, taking up the challenge. He hadn't moved from his position a few feet in front of the stage. 'You think I'm afraid of you? Fuck you. I knew you weren't treating us fair.'

The statement seemed to energize Dave Candon. He'd been standing inertly, looking on, not knowing whether to say anything or do anything. He reacted very deliberately, taking a short step down off the stage, and then walking over beside Greg, ready to step between the two men. It was a good thing he did, because Duane had heard enough. He lunged past Jones, pushing him out of the way and stepping off the stage. That brought him within reach of Greg. He brought his left hand up forcefully, intending to grab Greg by the throat. His right hand was cocked in a tight fist, ready at his side. Greg took a step back and threw up his right arm to shield himself. At the same instant, Dave Candon quickly moved between Greg and Duane, taking the full force of Duane's left arm on his shoulder and chest. He stumbled backward onto Greg. Meanwhile, Jones had stepped down off the stage and into the fracas, using both hands to grab and restrain Duane's right arm. With a murderous scowl on his face, Duane easily pulled his arm free and gave Jones a violent push. And then, suddenly, Duane just stopped. He dropped his arms and for a brief moment, just stood there. Maybe it was catching sight of Dave Candon, clear-eyed and slight, a pacifist if there ever was one, scared out of his mind, looking at him in such great despair. Maybe it was hearing Jones, emphatically urging them to stop: 'Come on, guys. Break it up. Let's cool down.' Maybe Duane just didn't want to waste his energy. In any event, he stopped; stopped flailing his arms, stopped pushing, stopped trying to get at Greg. He turned away

49

from the other three men and walked back up onto the stage, strapping on his Stratocaster and sitting down on his stool. As he played a few notes and adjusted the volume switch on his guitar, he looked back at Greg and the other two men in front of him. For a few seconds, the men just stood there, close together, disoriented and exposed, looking toward Duane. They looked as if they had just performed a piece of bad, amateur slapstick and now anxiously awaited the audience reaction. Duane's cold, monotone voice broke the short silence. 'Take your stuff and get the fuck out of here, Mazur.'

Jones wisely offered Greg his assistance. 'Hey, Greg' he said. 'Just head out to your car. I'll bring your amp and your mike stand out.' Wasting no time, Dave Candon shepherded Greg toward the door.

Greg stopped as he was walking out and looked back at Duane. 'You owe me a hundred bucks, Duane.' Dave Candon was right on Greg's heels and nudged him on to the door and out.

The last word went to Duane, spoken dismissively to the backs of Greg and Dave.

'Fuck you, Mazur.'

Greg Mazur was right. Not that it was going to do him any good. No one was going to congratulate him for exposing Duane's underhanded ways. And Duane certainly wouldn't be sending him a compensatory cheque. But the facts were these: the total annual cost for the band's website and domain-name was thirty-five dollars. And no accountant had been hired to file a tax return on behalf of the band, not that year or any other year.

The cost for the website was simply for memory space. It was a bare-bones website that Loretta had first created and published several years earlier, using a free program. She had proudly designed two websites at roughly the same time; one for her home sewing work and one for Duane's band. And she did any occasional updates that were required, easily and quickly, and free of charge.

As for the accounting, there was no "band tax-return"; there never had been. All Duane did was claim his individual income from the band's gigs on his own tax return. Actually Loretta did, as she was the one to file both their returns. She had long before insisted that Duane claim the income honestly, knowing it was his name that was listed on the agencies' accounts. She had no trouble reducing the taxable amount to zero with legitimate expenses. As for the other band members, present and past, they were on their own. Duane simply gave them their share from gigs and that was that.

The frequency with which Duane skimmed a piece off the top would have surprised even Greg Mazur. Maybe other band members had been aware of it in the past, or strongly suspected it, but Greg Mazur was the first to have actually called Duane out. Duane always had his half-baked excuses ready just in case. The real point was that it was Duane's band and always had been. If he thought an expense was justified, he didn't need to consult with anybody about it. If a gig originated directly through the band's website or by a phone call, he would claim a booking fee for himself. Just like an agent would. If he took a little extra for himself at times, it was because it was his band. He never said anything about these things to the rest of the band, and had absolutely no problem justifying the practices to himself. As for Greg Mazur, Duane's attitude was that people like him would bitch and complain no matter what you did.

Both Greg and Duane cooled off quickly once Greg had left the community centre. Neither man let the hostility eat away at him for very long. You just had to move on. When Greg got back to his Langside Street apartment that night, the first thing he did was crack open a beer. The second thing he did was check out Bandmix. He was looking for a new band. Duane left the community centre a little after the others, staying behind to play on his own. When he got home, he had a beer and checked out Bandmix. He was looking for a new lead vocalist.

5 Follow The Guitars

October 9

Ricki Clark's path to rock and roll may have been a straight line, but it was anything but free and easy. She was raised by a guitar-playing single father in Winnipeg's rough Point Douglas area. A quiet, solitary child, she obsessively emulated her dad and by the time she was twelve years old, she was playing her very own electric guitar, amazing the privileged few friends she was willing to play for. But as well as she could play, the world of bands and rock and roll was almost uniformly a male world. Girls that wanted to play lead guitar were unheard of. Finding sex-obsessed teenage boys who would treat her like a peer was hard enough, but the fact that she was better than almost anyone who heard her made it virtually impossible. After high school, the closed doors and disappointment continued, but she single-mindedly persevered, playing by herself at home and in her own small circle. Finally, in her early twenties, she met the right people, and joined an all-male band willing to give her a shot. She'd never looked back.

By the time Greg met Ricki for the first time, auditioning for her band Soul Doubt, she was a canny and talented thirty-year-old blues rocker. She was short - five foot two - and of medium build, with short brown hair and big, round, searching brown eyes.. Her overall appearance was plain and mostly unadorned; she usually wore slacks or jeans and a button-up shirt, along with a pair of black boots or black leather shoes. Greg was immediately impressed by how strong and independent-minded she seemed, though there was a definite wariness to her too, like she couldn't and wouldn't completely trust anybody.

Greg had never heard her play before, but Winnipeg was a small city, and he had certainly heard of her. She was "the woman who played lead". But their paths had never crossed; she was ten years younger than him and her bands had tended to play gigs for younger audiences.

It didn't take long for Ricki's playing to make a major impression on Greg. One of the first songs he auditioned was Stevie Ray Vaughan's *Pride and Joy*. Ricki's playing was phenomenal, screaming out the long solo part on her Stratocaster like she was born for it.

In his first several weeks with the band, Greg had a lot of unfamiliar songs to absorb and learn. As a result, he and Ricki spent a lot of time together, going through chords and arrangements, meeting in the evenings between practices. Yielding to the sure-fire combination of close proximity and raw sexual desire, they were sleeping together before long. He was only months removed from his most recent failed relationship; she hadn't been intimate with a man for a few years. While it was a situation they had fallen into without a lot of thought, they nonetheless forged ahead, jointly plotting their strategy for the awkward complications they would surely face with the band.

It was more than Ricki's highly sexual nature and aggressive lovemaking that drew Greg to her. She was unlike any woman he'd ever been involved with. She was so consistently straightforward and open in the way she lived and the way she communicated. And she was so self-sufficient. But in no time, the same qualities which attracted Greg to her him made him intensely jealous, and needlessly insecure. After all, she didn't really need him; not for financial support, not for any help in maintaining her home, and certainly not for emotional stability. She'd been doing just fine without him. Greg became obsessive in the way he watched her in her interactions with other men, in pitching as reasonable his questions to her about the time she spent apart from him. But he was a helpless victim of his jealousy. How many other bands had she been in where she was the only woman, he wondered? She had probably fallen for other men just like she'd done with him. Of course she had. And kept it to herself, just like she was doing now in relation to the rest of their band. She never talked to him about other men, about past lovers. She simply refused to talk about them. That was the past, she answered when he pressed her, it had nothing to do with the two of them. She made no commitments to Greg for the future. For the present, he was welcome to stay with her and share a lot of her life, but she insisted he keep his own apartment.

In Greg's past relationships, he had always considered himself completely normal in the extent to which he was jealous or possessive; in the way he'd regarded his girlfriends as being *his*, and in the loyalty he expected. But he had always held the emotional power in those relationships; his girlfriends needed *him*; they depended on *him*. He was the one controlling the situation. He would always be the one walking away when it didn't work out, not her. But Ricki was entirely different. She really liked him, and really lost herself in lovemaking with him. But she didn't *need* him and most of the time it seemed like he didn't really matter that much to her. The way he saw it, if he suddenly stopped coming over or found someone else, she wouldn't have even batted an eye.

By October of 2017, Greg's jealousy was approaching disastrous proportions. His constant interrogations of Ricki had become more than excessive; they had become psychotic. It wasn't just the time Ricki spent apart from him, or the ways she interacted with other male musicians, it was also the men she encountered at work. Her day job was at a small insurance agency, where she and three other women mindlessly processed home insurance and vehicle insurance policies, printing off forms and marking X where the customer had to sign. Her boss was a man and many of her customers were male. To Greg, this was highly fertile ground for suspicion. How often did she see her boss? When they went out for staff events, what did he say to her? Did he ever come on to her? How about the clients? They must have checked her out pretty closely all the time. He'd bought insurance. He knew how friendly the agents could be. Maybe she was paying some of her affections to one of the male clients...

For the moment, Greg and Ricki's relationship was hanging on, but the positive energy was steadily disappearing. Greg pressed and pulled; Ricki recoiled and moved farther back.

Into this troubled atmosphere came an innocent series of Monday night guitar lessons. Like many lead guitar players, Ricki played slide guitar only infrequently, and with mixed results. Aside from the basic mechanics, she knew little about technique and even less about the possible tunings she might employ. It was a skill she had long wanted to improve and, as the band was playing more blues numbers now, she felt it was a good time to work on it. She arranged lessons with a legendary guitar teacher in the city named Johnny La Montina.

Johnny La Montina was still going strong at 64 years of age. Except for his silver-coloured hair, which he slicked straight back, his appearance had barely changed over the years. With a toothpick clenched between his teeth, and his trademark Fu Manchu moustache, he was still trim and fit-looking. And he still wore a black t-shirt with a pack of cigarettes tucked under one sleeve. Over the years, he had performed in musical groups from every part of the spectrum: from country and western to psychedelic rock to grunge to folk music to alt-jazz. He had first made a name for himself in two popular Winnipeg rock bands in the seventies: Pete and the Pirates and Northern Comfort. But his enduring notoriety was due to his extraordinary talents as a guitar teacher. Among his more famous students were Randy Bachman, Kurt Winter and Brad Roberts. He had stopped performing at the age of 60 and now gave lessons full-time, five nights a week, driving his captive upstairs neighbours crazy.

For Ricki Clark, Monday, October 9 was her third lesson with Johnny La Montina. Despite the fact that Johnny looked like a small-time hustler, Ricki immediately felt comfortable with him. He had a quiet, patient manner and from their first meeting, made her feel like a long-time collaborator. In their first two lessons, Johnny emphasized the size and feel of the slide itself, as well as the importance of open tunings on the top strings. Each lesson, Ricki copied Johnny in playing a series of short exercises for slide, first slowly and then at an increased speed. Then Johnny asked her to fit each exercise into a short, improvised solo. Then the two of them would jam for five or ten minutes. All playing was recorded for Ricki to review at home. The lessons usually ran an hour and a half, ending with a friendly chat.

Ricki was an instant convert to Johnny La Montina's methods. At the end of each lesson, all she wanted to do was rush home and diligently practice. Greg was less enthusiastic. At first, although he hadn't actually encouraged Ricki, he had at least acknowledged that the lessons were a good idea; good for her playing and good for the band. But once the lessons actually started, it bothered him how friendly Ricki and Johnny seemed to be. Ricki was at her wits' end in trying to manage Greg's jealousy. She had a difficult time in answering his questions directly without provoking him.

At home after the first lesson, Greg tried to sound perfectly innocent in asking Ricki about it. 'So, what did you guys talk about? Did he tell you anything about the bands he'd been in?'

Ricki clearly saw the red flag and was careful in her response, partially lying to try and cut the conversation short. 'No, he didn't. I told him about the band we're in and the kind of music we play; the guitars I use. We didn't have much time to talk.'

'What kind of guitar was he playing?'

'A PRS model. I've seen them around, but I've never played one.'

'He must have a lot of guitars, I guess.'

'His whole room was full of them, lining the walls. He -'

'You were in his room?'

'Not *his room*, Greg. The room where he gives lessons. The living room or whatever. It's the main floor of a duplex, kind of one big room. He had guitars lining two of the walls, on stands at one end. Three or four Fenders, a Gretsch, a Rickenbacker, a few Gibsons. A number of acoutics too - a Gibson, a Martin. Some of them were older; some of them looked new. Pretty impressive.'

'Is he living with somebody? Is he married?'

'He said he's been living on his own for years.'

'He told you that?'

'Yes, he told me that?'

'I thought you said you never talked?'

'Fuck, Greg. Why do you always do this? We *didn't* talk. When I walked in, I said something like "You've got a nice place here", just to be polite. Then he said "It's small, but for one person, it's all I need. I moved in here about fifteen years ago. It's a good area, pretty good neighbours. The people above me put up with the noise, so that's good." That's all that was said, okay?'

A similar tone marked the conversation following Ricki's second lesson. That evening, Greg returned from his cab-driving shift around eleven-thirty. His last fare was out to the airport, so five dispiriting hours of cab-driving were followed by more driving; the long trek back to Ricki's place in Southdale: Route 90 to Bishop Grandin to Lakewood Boulevard. Lots of time to think about Ricki's lesson that night. He didn't trust Johnny La Montina; the guy was probably an old *letch*. Not married, in the music scene... he was probably around women all the time. Why wouldn't he play around with whoever he could?

Ricki lived in a comfortable, two-story, side-by-side, which had been her home for the past five years. When Greg walked in the door, she was sitting in front of the television, her Gibson in hand and her amp at a very low volume, half-watching the news.

'Hi' said Ricki, as Greg walked in, threw off his jacket and sat down on the sofa beside her. 'I was just watching the news.' She put her guitar down and turned the TV volume up. 'Harvey Weinstein.'

Greg took a quick glance at the TV and then impatiently asked Ricki about the lesson. 'So how did it go tonight?'

'Fine' Ricki answered, her flat tone clearly indicating she had no interest in an extended conversation on the subject. 'Are you hungry?'

'Not really. I picked up a burger at Junior's around 7, between fares.'

Watching the news, they briefly fell silent. Dustin Hoffman was the latest celebrity to be accused of sexual harassment.

'These men are horrible' said Ricki. 'I'm glad they're getting their names dragged through the mud. It's about time. Big shots. They've got all that power and money. So they treat women any way they want.'

'I'm not so sure about all this' said Greg, making conversation, but wanting to talk further about Ricki's lesson. 'The fat guy, sure. But all these other guys? What are they accused of? Speaking inappropriately? Groping? I think it's going way too far. Think of the first time you and I made out. I was about to leave and you got up to see me out. We were standing right over there. And then I just kind of grabbed you and kissed you on the lips. And I told you I thought you were really sexy and that you were driving me crazy. And then we got into it... Well, that could have been called "groping you" or "saying inappropriate things to you". I didn't know how you were going to react. I hoped you were into it, but...'

'There's a huge difference, Greg. Huge. I *wanted* you to touch me. I *wanted* you to tell me how you felt about me. We'd spent the evening together, we were both communicating in a sexual way all night.'

'But you never said anything or did anything. I did. I made the big move.'

'I know you did. But I wanted you to. That's the whole difference.'

'But I didn't know that. I hoped you did. But I didn't really know. What if you hadn't? Then I could have been accused of the same thing. And believe me, it's happened to me. You come on to a woman you're attracted to; she wants nothing to do with it and it ends right there. It happens to everybody. It happens all the time.'

'These are women whose jobs and careers were at stake if they didn't go along with the men. It's not the same situation at all, Greg.'

'What about a guy like Johnny La Montina?'

'What? What are you talking about, Greg?'

'Johnny La Montina. Your guitar teacher.'

'I know who he is, Greg. What are you trying to say?'

'He could do the same thing.'

60

'He's not like that. He's a very respectful man.'

'How do you know? Maybe you don't even know it. Maybe he'll think you're encouraging him or something?'

'You don't have to worry about it, Greg. I can take care of myself.'

'You might think you're just being friendly and he's thinking it's a green light.'

'Greg, you don't have to worry about it. Really. Nothing like that is going to happen. He's showing me things on guitar. It's very structured. and like I said, he is very respectful.'

'That doesn't mean it's not turning him on; sitting there staring at you.'

'Greg. He's giving me guitar lessons, okay? Nothing like that is going to happen. It's a comfortable, professional atmosphere. And I'm learning from him. There's nothing to worry about. He's a well-known, sixty-four-year-old guitar teacher. He doesn't have such a good reputation for nothing. I'm just another guitar player that wants a few lessons.'

'How do you know he's sixty-four?'

'He told me.'

'He told you?'

'Yah. When I first met him. I told him how long I'd been playing and how I'd heard about him, and he - '

'Sounds pretty personal to me. Like I said, you - '

Ricki had reached her limit with Greg's uncontrolled jealousy and the destructive course that the conversation was taking. 'That's it. This conversation is over, Greg. I'm tired. I'm going to bed. Give your head a shake, Greg. You're starting to do some real harm with these types of conversations. Don't you see that? I'm going to bed.'

Somewhere, way down in the sensible, rational part of Greg's psyche, he recognized that he shouldn't be threatened by Ricki's time with Johnny La Montina. For one thing, Ricki had never given him any reason to mistrust her. And secondly, Johnny was an old bugger. Ricki was definitely not into older men. But Greg couldn't help himself. His obsessive jealousy wouldn't go away. In the days following, the most he could do was try to conceal it. Most importantly, he had to conceal his developing plan for the next Monday, when Ricki would attend her third lesson.

In the early evening of October 9, four people converged on Johnny La Montina's North River Heights duplex: three guitar players and the wife of a fourth guitar player. In itself, this was hardly extraordinary, as Johnny's long suffering neighbours would quickly attest. And even the most perceptive observer, watching the comings and goings, could have had no idea as to the intense dramas playing out in front of him.

First to arrive was Greg Mazur, at 6:30. Highly charged and with binoculars at the ready, he intended to check out the proceedings at Johnny's when Ricki arrived. How did they greet one another at the door? How long would she be staying? Would the lights go out soon after the door closed behind her?

It was an ordinary work night for Greg, but he had made special arrangements with a co-worker. He had borrowed the man's unmarked Toyota Corolla for a few hours, leaving his far-too-noticeable cab at the office. No one would look twice at a five-year-old silver Toyota parked on the street. Greg had found the address on Johnny's website and cased the location over the weekend, scouting out a good place to park. The duplex was on a small, well-lit bay off Lanark Street, a few hundred yards from Academy Road. This made it possible for Greg to park inconspicuously on the opposite side of the bay from the duplex, with a perfect, unobstructed view. He had acquired the binoculars for a few dollars from a pawn shop near his cab company office.

It was a chilly fall night, around five degrees. On high alert as he anticipated Ricki's arrival, Greg left the Toyota running, listening to the radio with the lights off and the heater on. He took up the binoculars and carefully focused them on the door to Johnny La Montina's place. In the off-chance that Ricki might look over at him, Greg had donned a black touque, pulled down to his eyes.

Another guitar player drove into the bay, fifteen minutes after Greg had arrived. It was none other than Jimmy Green, the rhythm guitar player who had replaced Greg in The Drones. Jimmy and Greg had never met and Greg would probably have paid little attention to Jimmy's Jeep Wrangler if it hadn't pulled up right in front of Johnny La Montina's duplex.

Just like Greg, Jimmy had pulled into the bay because of Johnny La Montina. But Jimmy wasn't there for guitar lessons. Not exactly, anyway. Jimmy was there for the *pretext* of guitar lessons. This was his usual Monday night cover for meeting Loretta.

Jimmy had heard of Johnny La Montina through Duane. In Duane's band, much like every other band he'd played in, Jimmy's role was to play chords and sing vocals, mostly backup vocals. He had often thought to improve his picking, to be able to play some lead parts. Duane strongly encouraged him to seek out Johnny La Montina, the best guitar teacher in the city. Jimmy had thought about it seriously for a while. He even called Johnny to talk about his rates. But he never pursued the idea any further, settling in to his familiar role in the band.

When Jimmy and Loretta got involved, Jimmy saw the perfect excuse for getting out of the house to meet her: guitar lessons. Loretta was already attending yoga classes every Monday evening, so Monday evening became their night together. Jimmy's wife Karen knew he had been contemplating guitar lessons for some time; she'd even heard the name Johnny La Montina. So that became Jimmy's story. Except for necessary exceptions, like holiday weeks in the summer, on Monday nights, from 7 to 9:30, he would be taking lessons from Johnny. At 6:30 every Monday, he would leave his house, carrying his guitar, and drive off. Wanting to take no chances, Jimmy took the deceit a step further. He actually parked his jeep near Johnny's place every Monday night, waiting there until Loretta pulled up in her car to pick him up. Since Karen was home with the two girls, there was little chance she would be venturing out in the evening. But if she did, and if she happened to drive by the bay on Lanark Street, she would see his jeep there, just as it should have been. Loretta would drive him back to Johnny's a few hours later. From there it was a short drive to his and Karen's home, on Warsaw Avenue in Crescentwood.

Jimmy's vehicle was of little consequence for Greg's surveillance. Ricki had to walk up five stairs to reach the door of the duplex, so the view was still unimpeded. With his eyes trained for Ricki's impending arrival, Greg looked through his binoculars at the man getting out of the jeep. Kind of a shaggy-looking guy, with long hair and shades on. He was wearing a bomber jacket and cowboy boots. The man opened the rear door on the driver's side and pulled out what looked to be a guitar case. This he carried around to the back of the vehicle, where he opened the hatch and placed the case in the cargo area. After throwing a tarp or drop sheet over the case, he closed the hatch and then got back into the driver's seat.

In his anxious, hyper-jealous state, Greg's interest in the interloper was instantly transformed. What was this man doing there? At first, because of the guitar case, he thought the man must have had some connection to Johnny. Maybe he was waiting for the lesson before Ricki's to end, so he could meet with Johnny, maybe return a guitar. But why had he put the guitar in the back and covered it? Maybe it was Ricki. Maybe he was waiting for Ricki? Who was this guy?

Greg didn't have long to torture himself with the possibilities. Less than a minute later, a big, white Hyundai SUV pulled off Lanark and into the bay, stopping right alongside the jeep, directly between Greg and the jeep. At first, Greg didn't recognize the vehicle. The man had evidently been waiting for the SUV. He got out of his jeep and walked two steps toward the SUV, opening the door to get in. As he did, the interior light came on. In that split second, Greg clearly recognized the driver of the SUV. There was no doubt about it. It was Loretta Selby, her long brown hair tied back in a ponytail. It was a face and a vehicle he remembered well, from his years in Duane's band. He had seriously fancied Loretta himself for a while, but aside from a little teasing and flirting, nothing had happened between them.

The man, who Greg did not recognize, leaned over and kissed Loretta full on the lips. Then Loretta drove the SUV around the bay and back onto Lanark Street, passing right beside Greg before heading off toward Academy Road.

Well well well, thought Greg, suppressing a nasty chuckle. Loretta Selby... She must be stepping out on Duane. Ha! Good for her. That asshole deserves it.

But Greg had unfinished business to focus on. He took a deep breath and relaxed for a moment, then sat back and waited. Fifteen minutes later, Ricki drove up in her Honda Civic and parked in front of the jeep. She got out and walked up to Johnny's door, carrying her guitar case. She pushed the doorbell. The inside door opened and she walked in. Greg wasn't able to catch sight of Johnny. No other lights went on and none were turned off.

Greg slowly drove around to the other side of the bay, stopping for a moment right in front of the duplex, peering through the binoculars, but he was unable to see inside. He quickly looked over the jeep. It looked new. Its licence plate was R-O-C-K-O-N. Then he parked the car back where it had been and walked back along the sidewalk to Johnny's place, trying not to look too obvious. There were windows on either side of the door to Johnny's place, but the blinds were fully drawn on both. Greg had no other option but to retreat to his borrowed car and wait.

A little over an hour and a half later, Ricki emerged, carrying her guitar. Johnny was nowhere to be seen as she walked out onto the landing, down the stairs and over to her car. Greg waited until she left before driving off himself, to pick up his cab.

6 Monday Nights

September 25-October 2-October 9

October 9

After Jimmy jumped into the SUV, Loretta drove off toward Academy Road. She turned the volume down on *Not Alone Anymore*, a favourite song on her Roy Orbison mix. At seven in the evening, in light traffic, it was a quick, ten-minute drive from Johnny La Montina's duplex to Jimmy and Loretta's destination: over the St. James Bridge, west onto Portage Avenue, and south on Winston Road, to École Assiniboine.

The sprawling, red brick school was Jimmy's workplace, where he was responsible for janitorial and general maintenance duties. Its cramped little supply room office had been the site of all but two of Jimmy and Loretta's feverish trysts. Absolute secrecy was required, and the school's location fit the role perfectly. The east side of the school faced a large playground, bounded by a spruce forest separating it from the river. There wasn't a single residence or building that looked onto the playground from that side. Moreover, a person on foot could easily and innocently access the school property, via a narrow trail off Riverbend Crescent, where Loretta parked her SUV. Most evenings, the school grounds were completely empty, and Jimmy and Loretta could approach the school with no fear of inviting the slightest alarm or suspicion. Once there, a bare, gray delivery door, recessed near the middle of the school, provided a well-concealed entry point.

Conversations during those ten-minute drives had evolved over the year-plus that Jimmy and Loretta had been secretly meeting. For a long time, they were limited to simple expressions of lust and anticipation. Loretta would tell Jimmy how much she had missed him. Jimmy would tell Loretta how he'd been thinking about her all week. How much he wanted her. Jimmy would romantically hold Loretta's right hand, while she drove with her left on the wheel. As soon as they parked on Riverbend Crescent, they would devour each other with long, hungry, passionate kisses, before rushing off along the trail to the school.

Eventually, those snatches of conversation took on a predictable measure of small talk. By an unspoken agreement, inquiries and comments about ordinary domestic life were kept deliberately superficial. Jimmy's children's lives, Loretta's marriage, Jimmy's relationship with Karen - such things were never spoken of in any serious way. 'How was your week, Jimmy?' Loretta might ask, or 'How's work going?' 'The kids doing all right?' A few cursory syllables would rebound in response: 'Same old, same old' Jimmy might say, or 'Great. How about you, honey?' For the most part, these brief interludes passed easily and without tension.

But in the last several weeks, a darker, more problematic tone had established itself. At first, Jimmy hadn't been too troubled by Loretta's stormy, insistent outbursts. After all, they'd been involved for quite a while. It went with the territory, Jimmy thought, and Loretta's changeable emotional state was something he fully accepted. It was something he knew he had to manage and that he did manage. Pretty well, he thought. He'd always been able to provide enough re-assurance and physical affection to get through those tricky, testy moments.

No matter what had been said between them, no matter how Jimmy had been thinking about things when they were apart, he was crazy for Loretta. He was absolutely addicted to her body She was so beautiful, so unbelievably sexy. He couldn't wait to get his hands on her, to kiss her lips, to feel her body, to get his fingers inside her, to lick her, to watch her as she shook and moaned. To smell her, to taste her. All week, he couldn't get it out of his head; how he wanted to fuck her again and again. And then the day would come and that's exactly what would happen.

He found her totally irresistible. The way she made love to him; the way her body felt; the way she talked to him. Her voice was so raw and urgent, so driven, coming from another world. 'That's what you want, isn't it Jimmy?' she'd say. 'You want to fuck me, don't you Jimmy? Tell me. Tell me, Jimmy.' She was so uninhibited and direct. She would tell Jimmy exactly what she wanted. 'Tie my hands behind my back, Jimmy. Do what you want to me.'

Though fifty-one years of age, Loretta could have easily passed for thirty-five. She was five-foot eight; thin with small firm breasts, and long, sexy legs. She had long brown hair that she often tied back or braided. Her soft, green-brown eyes were magnetic; if she found you with a glance, you just couldn't look away; you didn't want to look away. She had gorgeous, flawless, pale skin, high cheek bones, a small, straight nose and perfect full lips. She usually wore red lipstick, with large, geometrically-shaped earrings, rings on both hands and a necklace or gold chain around her neck. Whether she was wearing a sleeveless cotton dress and sandals in the summertime, or tight blue jeans, black leather boots and a white cotton shirt in the winter, she looked absolutely ravishing. To Jimmy, her physical beauty fit perfectly with her tough, confident nature.

Their affair had been perfect; a perfect arrangement. It was what she wanted too, what they'd both agreed on, from the very beginning. There was an incredible, irresistible, undeniable physical attraction between them. Sex was *so* good. They were like a pair of wild, rabid dogs when they got together. Completely separate were their *real* lives:

69

their homes, their work, their partners, their routines. Loretta had lost her job at Sears two years earlier, and now her income depended on a home sewing business that she operated from her basement. In the summers, she diligently tended a large vegetable garden in the back yard. At the centre of Jimmy's life were his two precious young daughters and his hard-working, devoted wife. These, and all of the essential components of their lives, emotional and material, had continued in the same way, undisturbed, in parallel, and at the same pace.

Theirs were two worlds. One, the ordinary substance of day-to-day life, established long before, having nothing to do with each other. And second, the world of extreme, intense, sexual expression. They could have both worlds. That's what they were doing. That's what they both said they wanted. There was no need to destroy the predictable, secure parts of their lives or the routines that filled them. There was no need to blow up relationships. Those worlds, those lives, would continue, unharmed and unbroken. And regularly, secretly, they could give so much pleasure to each other. Every week, they could slake their hyper-intense sexual appetites in a world apart.

But not anymore. The artificial emotional distance they had maintained was no longer tenable. Small talk of any kind sounded ridiculous now. Lovemaking had felt much less free and much less satisfying for many weeks. Loretta's small outbursts had given way to fiery threats and troubling demands.

Two Mondays before, on September 25, Loretta had firmly and insistently stopped Jimmy as he began to take off her clothes. It was the first time she'd done anything like that, and it really jolted Jimmy and made him stop and think. They were in the supply room at the school. It had started out like any other Monday, with Jimmy's foam mat unrolled on the floor. They were standing near the door.

Jimmy had thrown off his jacket and was starting to unbutton Loretta's jeans.

Often they never even made it to the floor, not at first anyway. Jimmy would have Loretta from behind, standing up, with Loretta slightly bent over the cluttered wooden desk, fucking her so forcefully and so fast that he came within seconds. The second time, as soon as Jimmy was hard again, maybe then they used the mat. Though Jimmy just as often wanted her sitting on the edge of the desk, facing him, locking eyes, her legs extended and held up for him.

'Wait. Stop. Stop, Jimmy' Loretta had said intently, two weeks earlier, planting her hand forcefully against Jimmy's chest. 'We have to talk. I need to talk to you.'

'I want you so much' Jimmy answered, reaching for her again.

'I can't do this anymore' Loretta said, highly upset and drawing back from Jimmy. 'I mean, I want to be with you. I do. But I want more, Jimmy. I wanted to talk to you this week. I really needed to talk to you. And I didn't. I could have called you. Maybe I should have. I was going to, but I didn't. You don't even know what goes on in my life. It doesn't even matter to you. You just don't care. This is all you want and you're happy. But I need more than just fucking, Jimmy.'

Jimmy tried to calm her down. 'We've talked about this, Loretta' he said quietly. 'I *do* care about your life. Of course I do. You know that. But we have to be careful. We can't blow this. It's so good. You know why we don't call. Karen checks out my phone all the time. Mostly for pictures and stuff, but she -'

'I don't care what she does, Jimmy. Figure it out. Get another phone for fuck's sake. I want to talk to you sometimes. I want to have a real relationship. I want to have a meal together. I want to cook a meal for you,

71

Jimmy, and then get to enjoy it together. I just want to spend some ordinary time with you. Doing ordinary things. Maybe listen to some music or watch a movie. Or just hang out and talk. Have a glass of wine. Make it real.'

'Loretta, you know what we said about all that. We both agreed. Maybe we can figure out some way to spend some time on a long weekend. But we'd have to really figure it out. I'd have to have a real good reason to get away. I'd have to plan it and set it up and -'

Loretta was extremely fired up. She wasn't about to be placated. 'It's no good like that, Jimmy' she said angrily. 'That's just more of the same thing. Keep sneaking around... make up more lies. Just to get together and fuck. I want to be able to go out with you. Have an ordinary time. Talk about what's going on in the world...in my life. This is just-'

'Loretta, that's not what we're doing. We can't do that. We have to be smart about this. I have a wife and two daughters. I'm not going to do anything that - '

'Anything honest? Face the truth? Why not? I know you have feelings for me, Jimmy. I know you love me. People can't be together like we are, every week, and not care about each other. I know it's hard, Jimmy. It's hard to think about. Your wife, your kids. You don't want anybody to be hurt. You don't want anybody's comfortable little world to change or get messed up. People deal with things like this all the time, Jimmy. And they do just fine. People move on. How cozy and comfortable would your wife's little world be if she knew what was going on? If she knew how you felt about me? If she knew how long you've been seeing me? How long you've been lying? I don't care what you say about loving your wife, Jimmy. You can't love her and be the way you are with me. It's just not possible. And your kids? And don't tell me I don't understand because I don't have kids. That is total bullshit. If you ever split with Karen, things would be just fine for them. Because you'd make sure they were. And I would be totally supportive. I would help you. We can - '

Jimmy was stunned by Loretta's anger and by her aggressive, challenging tone. He immediately shifted into a protective, defensive posture, trying to remain composed and not provoke Loretta any further.

'Loretta. Hold on a second. I know what you're saying. Of course things would be totally different if Karen knew. That's the whole point. I *haven't* told her anything. That's what we agreed on. That's why we've been able to see each other like we have. That's the only way it was going to work. We both understood that. And what about *your* world? What if Duane found out? He'd probably go completely nuts. I don't know what he'd do. Maybe he'd want to kill me. Or you. Or both of us. And wouldn't that be a great way for this to go? Come on, Loretta. I know you're upset, but let's be sensible. We're not going to do anything drastic like that. You're not going to tell Duane and I'm not going to tell Karen.'

'Oh yah? Maybe I'll tell Karen, Jimmy. Wouldn't that be nice, ay, if she heard it from me? Maybe I'll tell Duane, too. Maybe I'll tell them both. This isn't enough for me anymore, Jimmy. We've done this long enough. I love you. I want to have a real relationship with you.'

'That can't happen, Loretta. We agreed. That's not fair of you.'

'*Fair* of me? What the fuck is fair, Jimmy? Is your life fair?'

With those words, angry and disgusted, Loretta put on her jacket and turned to leave. 'Think about it, Jimmy' she said, collecting herself. 'Think about it seriously. I want to be with you. I want a real relationship with you.' She walked out the door of the supply room, leaving Jimmy behind. He'd have to walk back to Lanark Street.

73

Jimmy wanted to believe that Loretta was only trying to provoke him, wanting him to declare his feelings for her, to say he loved her. He wanted to believe that he could manage the situation somehow, by making some kind of small change or gesture. That her threats weren't serious threats. That her emotions were just a little out of control. That she would calm down and realize what was at stake. That things would return to normal. He *wanted* to believe those things but he couldn't. She was so angry, so strong-willed. The way she expected things to go... the kinds of threats she was making... It was crazy. But she meant it. Jimmy had no doubt about it. She was dead serious.

Anxiety filled the next several days for Jimmy; not knowing what to do, fearful of what Loretta might do. He was certain that Loretta was going to do something dramatic, to force the issue. Things were never going to be the same with her again, whether Jimmy wanted them to be or not. No matter what happened, he would never be able to trust her in the same way again. Even if Loretta suddenly came to her senses and experienced a complete change of heart. And Jimmy was under no illusions about that possibility. He was convinced Loretta was going to issue an ultimatum: either he had to take concrete steps to leave Karen or she would tell Karen about their affair.

What could he do? He had to get out of his relationship with Loretta entirely, that much was clear. But how? He couldn't simply break up with her. That would be like detonating a bomb. The first thing Loretta would do, would be to email Karen, or pay her a nice visit. She would do and say anything she could to ruin Jimmy's marriage and his family life. She would make sure Jimmy paid a heavy price. The only other way to end the affair was to slowly but deliberately bleed it to death, over time, until Loretta also wanted to walk away from it. But how was that even remotely possible, when Loretta was so out of control, making insane statements about wanting to have a real life with Jimmy, to help him raise his kids? It wasn't.

Was there any other feasible option? He could genuinely try to reason with Loretta, try to persuade her not to tell Karen, while somehow continuing the affair. But what could he possibly offer to placate her, to satisfy her? Wouldn't that eventually lead to the same prospect he was about to face now - an ultimatum to leave his wife?

Over the next few days, these fraught scenarios repeatedly ran through Jimmy's distracted and troubled mind. It was all he could do to meet the nominal demands and expectations of his day-to-day life. Talking with Karen, trying to appear interested in what she was saying. Pretending to be asleep so he wouldn't have to talk to her in bed at night. Relating to his two daughters on their level; trying to put on a brave and cheerful face. Driving them where they needed to go; to school, swimming lessons, friends' houses... Managing meals, shopping, going to work in the morning. Doing his job. At the same time, trying to hide his deep troubles from everyone.

Jimmy was tormented and afraid. It was dragging him down. And unless he did something, things were going to get a whole lot worse. He.knew he had to confront the situation in a decisive way.

Losing Karen, breaking his children's hearts, the destruction of his family - these horrific possibilities had never really occurred to Jimmy before. Everything had been so much under control. There was nothing to fear; he'd been so sure of it. If he'd ever thought of how things would go with Loretta in the long term, it was with minimal concern. One or the other of them - maybe both - would someday tire of the situation, the passion gone. One of them would bluntly tell the other it was time to call it a day. And it would be crystal-clear that it really was. When the intense thrill, the raw lust, the crazy need was no longer there... Maybe one of them would be more unhappy about it than the other, but it wouldn't take long to get over it. Life would go on.

But Loretta had absolutely blindsided him. Somewhere along the way, some major transformation had happened. Unless she'd been misleading him all along. Maybe she'd always thought that one day they'd be together, a real couple. Maybe she couldn't fake it anymore.

Jimmy realized there was no way out of it. Karen was going to find out, one way or another. So it should be from him. Maybe if he said the right things, told Karen a trimmed-down version of things, and sounded genuinely remorseful, things would be all right. Karen was a devoted wife and mother, through and through. And she didn't have a vengeful bone in her body. She'd want to keep the family together. She'd give Jimmy another chance. At least that was what Jimmy told himself, over and over.

But little by little, dark doubts began to creep into Jimmy's thoughts. What if Karen flipped out? What if she despised him for what he'd done and could never forgive him? What if she wanted nothing to do with him again? Maybe she'd want to kick him out. Or maybe she'd take the kids to her sister's place. Then she'd get a lawyer. It would be a nightmare. They'd all go through the meat grinder and then stagger out the other end - a broken family, burdened with money issues, lives poisoned by hostility and resentment.

And then there was Duane. It was impossible that he wouldn't find out, Jimmy thought. So much for the band... What would Duane do? Jimmy didn't have the slightest clue how he was supposed to handle that. Do nothing? Just sit around and wait for Duane to come and find him and mash his face? Talk to the guy? What could you possibly say?

Jimmy felt like a complete idiot, a total fool, for not having thought seriously about these things before. What was he going to tell Karen? How was he going to tell her? What was the best strategy? He didn't want to lose her. He didn't want to lose his family. And he sure didn't want to be another one of those guys who ends up in court; his wife taking him to the cleaners. Like his friend from work, Charlie Senchuck. Charlie was the gym teacher at Jimmy's school. At the beginning of the school year he'd confided in Jimmy, told him that he was trying to save his marriage. It hadn't gone well for Charlie. He was broken-down and alone. Throwing big money away on lawyers. His wife wanted the house and the kids. Charlie had to move out. He was living in a two-bedroom apartment in Westwood. Another teacher suggested to Charlie that he go to counselling - their contract provided for two free sessions with a marriage counsellor. So Charlie went. Once with his wife and once by himself. He told Jimmy it hadn't really helped.

Counselling. Jimmy thought it was all bullshit. Psychiatrists spouting off a pile of useless crap you could read on the internet for free. Two free appointments and then they kept you coming back, nicely taking your money off you. Thieves. But he had an idea. Maybe he could use counselling to his advantage. If he told Karen he'd been feeling terrible about what he'd done - for some time - and that he wanted to do anything he could to save their marriage and their family... but he'd been so afraid and didn't know what to do or how to talk to her... *and the proof was that he'd gone to counselling...* maybe it would make a difference to her; she'd believe him; believe that he really meant what he said. And he could actually go to a counsellor, for free through work, so he wouldn't be lying about it. He could put up with it for one appointment. He'd tell Karen the counsellor's name - Doctor so and so - and throw in a few buzz words. At least it was a plan. It couldn't hurt. Maybe it had a decent chance to work.

The next Monday, October 2, Jimmy's worst fears were confirmed. Loretta phoned him at work. When the call came, it was nearly noon. He was in the hallway outside the supply room, loading art supplies onto a large dolly. Seeing Loretta's name on the phone display sent a cold shock down Jimmy's spine. They had an iron-clad agreement not to call or text - ever - except if there was some huge emergency, which there never was.

Jimmy quickly tried to collect himself and not sound too irritated or disturbed. He walked back into the supply room and closed the door. 'Loretta? What's happening? I'm at work.'

'Hi honey. I had an idea. See, it's not the end of the world if I call you. Hard to believe, isn't it, Jimmy? Normal people do this all the time.'

Loretta's tone was cool and assertive, and slightly sarcastic, as if she was daring Jimmy to object.

'Loretta. You can't just call like this. You can't. We agreed.' As soon as Jimmy said this, he realized it was a mistake. Not only was it the wrong time and the wrong place to argue with her, it was counterproductive. He decided the best thing to do was to say as little as possible, just let Loretta say what she wanted.

'I want to change up where we go tonight. Just try something a little different.'

'What do you mean?'

'I want to meet for a drink. Just to feel what it's like. We can talk, have a couple of drinks. It'll be fun. Maybe we'll even have time for another kind of fun before you have to go home. I've kind of been missing you.'

'Loretta, we can't do something like that. What if - '

'The hell we can't. You'll see how easy it is. Don't worry so much, Jimmy. It'll be fun. It'll be like our first date, after all this time.'

'Loretta...'

'I guarantee a good time will be had by all. Let's meet at the King's Head at 7. Upstairs. Both bring our own cars.'

'The King's Head? Loretta, we played a gig there not too long ago. They know me there. They know Duane there. No way.'

'Okay, you pick a place.'

Jimmy knew he had little choice. He had to keep things cool until he figured out what he was doing. 'The Gold Rush.'

'The Gold Rush? Jeez, Jimmy, that's way out in Transcona.'

'That's the whole point. It's a country bar; a working man's bar. There's a pretty good chance no one will know either of us.'

'It's so far to go.'

'I'm trying to compromise here, Loretta. It's a lot shorter for you than it is for me. Just go down Main to Chief Peguis. That'll get you to Grassie. Then it's only a couple of minutes from there. It's just off Regent.'

'Okay. See you tonight at 7.'

'It'll be closer to 7:30. Remember, I leave the house between 6:30 and 7.'

'Maybe you can leave a little earlier. Okay, I'll see you there.'

Jimmy deleted the call, deleted the new contact created, and shook his head anxiously. It was snowballing, he thought, just like he was afraid it would. He was going to have to do something.

Fortunately or not, the rest of Jimmy's day was so busy he hardly had any time to dwell on the evening ahead, or what he was going to do about the situation. It was one thing after another at work: deliveries, repair jobs that couldn't wait, getting the gym floor done before the end of the day. He was fifteen minutes late picking up his daughters at their school in River Heights. Then his wife Karen called to say she'd be late, so he was on his own for dinner with the girls. Karen was an office assistant for a dental clinic on Stafford Street, and was in the middle of yet another change in their software. Jimmy warmed up leftovers for dinner, gabbed with the girls, and then quickly cleaned up and did the dishes. Karen walked in the door, exhausted, at 7:10. Jimmy had been watching the clock nervously and with barely a hello to Karen, immediately left for his Monday night guitar lesson.

No matter which way you went, driving out to Transcona from the west end of the city was always a major ordeal, with ridiculously heavy traffic and unavoidable road construction projects that had been going on for years. Finally, Jimmy made it across Highway 59. Next came the long, sobering drive down Regent. Past the huge malls, with the same depressing stores as thousands of other cadaverous city malls. Past the tawdry casino, where citizens eagerly gathered in their numbers, day in and day out, to throw their money away, straight into the grasping hands of their dutiful provincial government; always getting a chance to check out the B-list has-beens, like Lee Aaron or Foreigner or Loverboy. Finally, past the chicken joint at Hoka, then a right on Bond Street, and voilá, The Gold Rush. Despite its impressive name, the establishment looked dreary and subdued. It was a non-descript, single story building, with a heavy, metal-framed glass door at the front. Over the entrance, an old, faded, white marquee faced the street, bearing fixed black letters: *Oct 2-6 Rundle Mountain Band 8pm-12pm.*

Jimmy parked on the street and took a look around. There were very few cars parked nearby. As he got out of his jeep, he could hear a muffled version of whatever the band was playing, mostly the bass and drums. He took off his shades and tucked them away in the chest pocket of his leather jacket. By the time he walked into the place, it was ten minutes past eight. He'd had lots of time to think on the way out, to prepare for his special date. He was going to be patient; disciplined; keep his emotions in check; not get drawn into hostile arguments. He would try not to push Loretta's buttons. Play it cool for now.

The Rush, as locals had always called it, was an old-time, country-music dive. Walking in the door, you were instantly hit with the disgusting, stale stench of years of weak draft beer and cigarette smoke. It was the kind of place where your shoes stuck to the floor. A few small pool tables stood at one end. Along a wall in the middle of the room was a raised stage, facing over a dancing area, with a long bar on the opposite side of the floor. Small round tables with molded laminate tops and metal-legged chairs lined the dancing area and filled the rest of the room. It was a blue-collar bar whose better days were long gone. But you could still hear live music there, even on a Monday night.

On this night, The Rundle Mountain Band, out of Calgary, had just started their first set of the night, gamely performing country and western covers to an almost empty place. No more than six tables were occupied. Jimmy took a quick, nervous look around. There was Loretta, at a table close to the stage, her hair down, looking beautiful, soaking up the attention from the middle-aged men checking her out from the other tables. She was working on a tall rum

81

and coke, looking like she'd been coming to the place all her life.

Loretta had her back to the door and didn't notice Jimmy until he was nearly right at her table. He sat down in the chair beside her. 'Hi Loretta' he said, his voice all but drowned out by the band. 'Hey, where's my kiss?' she answered, speaking loudly enough to be heard, leaning over toward him with an inviting smile. Jimmy responded with a quick kiss. She stayed where she was until he kissed her again, the second time a longer, sweeter kiss.

As anxious as Jimmy was about the possibility of being seen by someone, as resolved as he was about Loretta, one look at her and he was a goner, right back under her spell. She was wearing blue jeans and a black turtleneck, with a turquoise gemstone on a silver chain around her neck. In the dim light of the bar, Jimmy couldn't take his eyes off her. As he'd told her before, she was the kind of woman he always used to notice in a place - at a party or in a bar or walking down the street - and wonder why he never got to meet anyone that beautiful.

It was a very good five-man country band, and despite the sparse crowd, they weren't holding anything back. Except for the lead vocalist, a young blonde-haired man who looked to be in his thirties, the rest of the band looked to be in their late fifties or older. After Jimmy ordered a Keith's, the band laid into *If I Needed You*, with an old guy in a cowboy hat playing an incredible intro on pedal steel. Both Jimmy and Loretta just sat back and listened for the rest of the set, Loretta clapping after every song, with the waiter coming back a few times to push more drinks. Neither Jimmy or Loretta had heard of the band, but they were both highly impressed. After doing terrific versions of *Your Cheatin' Heart* and *Oh Lonesome Me*, they left Hank Williams and Townes Van Zandt behind and played Dwight Yoakum's *Fast As You*.

82

'That guitar line sure sounds like *Pretty Woman* by Roy Orbison' said Loretta at the end of the song, playfully indignant. 'Roy could have sued.'

Jimmy looked on in admiration as the band sailed through their set. He'd been in the same situation many times, playing to a depressing, empty house. You had to forget about it and just play; try not to treat the situation like a joke. In situations like these, the front man had to resist saying things like "I want to thank you for coming out, both of you..." or "Tonight would be a great night to buy everyone a round of drinks. But I'm going to be strong and resist the urge anyway..."

It was only after the set ended that Loretta and Jimmy talked. 'This is nice, Jimmy' said Loretta. 'See, it's not so hard. Come on, now. I'm not such a bad date.' She held up her glass to clink with Jimmy's beer. 'Cheers. How was your day, Jimmy?'

Jimmy knew the other shoe was going to fall any minute. 'Not bad. Real busy at work. How about you, Loretta?'

Loretta locked eyes with Jimmy and smiled her sexy, killer smile, and took Jimmy's hand in hers. Jimmy quickly jerked his band back. 'Sorry, Loretta, Can we not...' he said, not bothering to finish the sentence.

'No P-D-O-A?' said Loretta. 'Public displays of affection? That's what we used to call it: P-D-O-A. Jeez, Jimmy. Relax. Nobody knows you in this place.' She laughed. 'It's not like I'm reaching for your crotch.'

Loretta finished her rum and coke and signalled to the waiter for another, holding up the glass and pointing to it. 'Another beer, Jimmy?'

'No thanks, I'm good' Jimmy answered. 'I have to be at work at 7:30.'

'Okay. I'll finish my drink fast, so we can head for the school.'

'I'd really like to Loretta, but it's too late. It's past 9 already. By the time we get there and - '

'Hey, we've got the car. The back seat of my SUV was good to us before. Remember? The second time we were ever together.'

'Loretta, maybe tonight we should just -'

'Come on, Jimmy. I want you to fuck me. Can't you tell? I've wanted you all week. We can be really fast. So what if you're home half an hour later? You can think of an excuse. The lesson was longer.'

It was all Jimmy could do to resist. Despite everything, looking at Loretta, the way she was looking at him, the way she was talking, Jimmy wanted her. It wouldn't have taken a whole lot of convincing. The thought flashed through Jimmy's head of following Loretta into the women's bathroom, pulling her jeans off and fucking her against the wall. But he managed to control himself and dispel the thought. For a few awkward seconds, he simply sat looking at Loretta, saying nothing. Loretta picked up on his reluctance and backed off a little. 'I like this, Jimmy' she said, looking around the mostly empty bar. 'Being out with you. I like it a lot. Did you think about what we were talking about last week? About a real relationship?'

'I did, Loretta' Jimmy answered, unsurprised at the sharp turn in the conversation. 'I want to ask you something' he said, trying to choose his words carefully. 'What changed? Did something change? I mean, things have been rolling on. Things have been good. And then, it seems like you changed. It kind of came out of nowhere for me. Maybe you can tell me why - '

Loretta interrupted, in an irritated, impatient tone. 'Why? What changed? I'll tell you what changed, Jimmy. I fell in love with you, that's what. I don't know, maybe I was just scared to tell you for a while. I deserve a chance to be with someone I love, Jimmy. And so do you.'

Jimmy looked around a little nervously. Even though no one was near them, he still felt very conspicuous. 'Loretta, can we keep this down?' he said, motioning with his hands for her not to be too loud.

Loretta changed gears, offering an affectionate entreaty. 'You have no idea how good I could be for you, Jimmy. How good we could be *together*. I could be *everything* for you.' And then, in an instant, her tone changed back again and she sounded angry and indignant. 'And don't tell me that you were happy enough before I came along, with your wife and your kids and your school job and your white bungalow and your rock and roll music... Because I know you weren't. Because you wanted *me*. It's not like you just wanted to get laid a few times and then so long, honey. I mean, think about it, Jimmy. How long have we been doing this? You weren't happy either. I know I can make you happy. Sure it feels good to have a nice familiar home and a wife who probably works herself to the bone for you, two great children that love their daddy... But that's not happiness. That's just security; security and predictability. Happiness is something you feel in your soul. It's not when you're looking around for someone else to get you by, not when you're lying all the time to hide something that matters so much. I know you love me, Jimmy. And I know it's hard for you to tell me. I know you're scared. But there's two of us in this together. I want a real relationship with you. If you were being honest with your wife - if you were being honest with yourself - we wouldn't even be having this conversation. And you know something, Jimmy? I bet she already knows. Maybe she's known for a long time. Do you think you can hide from someone who's been living with you for so long? Do you think you can just waltz in the door at ten o'clock, smelling like pussy, jump into bed and she doesn't notice anything? Are you kidding me? Oh, sorry; maybe you shower as soon as you get in the house. Is that what you do? Don't you think she'd wonder why you shower every time you have a guitar lesson? She *must* know. She's probably too humiliated to do anything about it, or too scared and confused to figure out what to do. Anyway, that's not for me to say, Jimmy. I just don't want to be a side attraction anymore. I give you everything when we're together. I just want a chance at a real relationship with someone I love. Everything's possible, Jimmy. We're in this together. You figure out a way to get it moving. It doesn't have to happen all at once, over night, but you have to make a start, a real start. If you can't, I can.'

Jimmy just sat there, listening uncomfortably, getting his ears severely pinned back, realizing that at some point, he was going to have give some kind of answer. By the time Loretta finished, she was just as aggressive and demanding as she had been the previous week. If she thought she was provoking Jimmy into some kind of positive action, she couldn't have been more wrong. All she'd done to Jimmy was push him away, doubly reinforcing his conviction to escape from the situation.

'Loretta, I hear what you're saying, all right? I can't just change, like that. You have to give me a chance to think about all this. It's a complete change you're talking about - '

'Figure it out, Jimmy. Like I said, she probably knows already, anyway. You just have to face it. Figure out how to talk to her about it. I know it's hard. But you have to be honest. She deserves that from you. We'll be so good together, Jimmy. We - '

This time it was Jimmy interrupting, uneasily looking at the time on his iPhone. 'Sorry, Loretta' he said. 'I don't want to be a jerk, but I have to head back. I *have* to. I hear what you're saying. Please, you have to let me think about it. Can we meet next week as usual, at Lanark?'

The long drive home was anything but calming for Jimmy. Past the casino and its packed parking lot again, plodding through the mall traffic, one red light after another. His thoughts were even more troubled now than they'd been on the way out. He knew for sure that Loretta wasn't going to back off or radically change her mind -not that he'd really had much doubt about it. That meant there was only one thing he could do; one thing he *had* to do. He was going to have to make his case to Karen. He really didn't believe she knew about the affair, as Loretta had suggested. The first thing would be to make an appointment with a counsellor. Then he'd figure out what he'd say to Karen and when. Until then, he would say nothing to Loretta, just put her off if he had to, deflect things, play along with her to a certain extent. He'd tell Loretta after he'd talked to Karen, tell her it was over between them.

Having a rough strategy, a plan, offered only a brief moment of relief. Then the same panicky scenarios pressed back into the front of Jimmy's thoughts. What was Loretta going to do when he told her? Would she try to ruin his life? What about Duane? What would happen if *he* found out? *When* he found out? Would Duane come after him? Was there a physical risk to his family, to his home? When and how would he leave the band? Would he make up some lame excuse to take his amp home after one of the next few practices? Then what? Should he talk to Duane directly about it, too? Would it make sense to email him? Or should he just say nothing at all to Duane? And above everything, what would Karen do? How would she react?

No matter how he tried to imagine the best possible outcome, Jimmy knew that three other people were involved, people whose reactions were unpredictable and totally beyond his control. Someone or something was bound to blow up at some point.

Jimmy drove on. He told himself to calm down. He had to keep it together, and try not to think of everything all at once. He'd just have to get through it, that's all. Have a little faith that things would work out. He was scared.

It was pure insanity. As overwhelming as everything was, with a series of potential catastrophes looming, still, one potent image kept coming back to Jimmy, drawing him on; Loretta's face, the way she'd looked at him when she said 'Come on, Jimmy. I want you to fuck me.' He couldn't get it out of his head, and he wanted her every time it reappeared.

On Monday, October 9, the short drive from Johnny La Montina's was an extraordinary study in deception. Loretta had more or less made up her mind to leave Duane. She'd been quietly, deliberately, hatching a plan; what she'd say to Duane, where she'd go in the short term, right after telling him, what she'd say to Jimmy and when. But she said nothing of this to Jimmy. Jimmy was also harbouring a momentous secret. After returning home the previous Monday night, he had stopped waffling and made up his mind. He had set up a counselling appointment, paid for by the school division, for October 13. Following that appointment, he would tell Karen about his affair with Loretta; that it was over now and that he'd gone to counselling. That he was willing to do anything to save their marriage and their family. He'd have faith in Karen and squarely face the consequences. After he told Karen, he would end it with Loretta the next time he saw her.

Like Loretta, Jimmy intended to say nothing about his secret plan that night. He had made up his mind to just play along with Loretta, and not provoke her. He fully expected her to pressure him again, to demand some kind of action on his part. When she did, he would try to deflect her questions and expectations to some extent, but he would make sure not to look too obvious. He'd lie if he had to.

It was a masterful performance by both participants. Both came off as genuinely affectionate and ready for some lovemaking. The atmosphere in the white SUV seemed tension-free. Each found it easy to mirror the tone of the other. To Loretta, Jimmy was more than sufficiently solicitous. To Jimmy, the way Loretta looked at him and spoke to him felt entirely comfortable and, at least temporarily, without pressure.

'I've missed you Jimmy. All week. Mmm. I can't wait to fuck you. It's been too long.'

'I've missed you too. You look beautiful.'

'Thanks. You look pretty good yourself. I brought you a treat, Jimmy.'

'Oh yah? Great! Are you going to tell me what it is?'

'Two treats, actually. The first treat is me, Jimmy. I can't wait to give it to you. But I have an ordinary kind of treat, too. For after... A big slice of pumpkin pie, with whipping cream. I made a pie for Thanksgiving.'

'Great! I love pumpkin pie.'

'Aren't you going to ask me about Thanksgiving? Neither of us said anything about it last week. That's kind of ridiculous. Did you have a big turkey dinner?'

'We had Karen's sister and her family over yesterday. Karen cooked a huge turkey. How about you?'

'We went out yesterday. We went to Duane's brother's place. Duane's brother is his best friend. We get together with his brother's family quite a lot.'

'I don't think I've met his brother.'

'Ralph's his name. You might have met him. He's been at a few of your gigs. He's got a crewcut. He's a lot taller than Duane.'

'So dinner went okay?'

'Not bad. Did you have to make up a different excuse for tonight?'

'No. Johnny gives lessons every weekday, no matter what, except when Christmas falls on a weekday. He told me that when I called him about lessons. So it's just another

Monday. How about you? Are there yoga classes on Thanksgiving Monday?'

'No classes today. But it's different for me. I just walk out the door. All I have to say is I'm going out for a while. He'd never bat an eye.'

Loretta pushed the select button a few times on the stereo and glanced over at Jimmy. 'Hey, listen to this. I found this on the internet. You're not going to believe it. Keith Richards, solo, playing keyboard and singing *All I Have To Do Is Dream*.'

'That's *three* treats' said Jimmy with a smile, as the song began to play.

When they parked on Riverbend, Jimmy and Loretta kissed. It was a long, sexy kiss. Loretta leaned over, removed Jimmy's sunglasses and held him, with her right hand around the back of his head. Jimmy didn't have to try too hard to get into it. Then Loretta retrieved a plastic container with the pie from the backseat, and they walked quickly along the trail to the school, where Jimmy unlocked the grey delivery door.

Jimmy couldn't pull off his cowboy boots and his jeans fast enough. It had been three long weeks since he'd last had Loretta. And despite all the tension and anxiety that had marked those days, he had imagined it again and again; fantasized about it; couldn't stop thinking about it. He knew it had to end. He had to stop. But here he was and he was powerless.

As if it made any difference, Jimmy had bolstered his twisted conscience with two convincing rationales. One, that it was actually necessary: he had to play along with Loretta and act like he usually would. Above anything, he couldn't provide even the smallest hint that something was up, that he had a plan. If Loretta picked up any scent of treason, she would surely tell Karen before he did. And then, what little control he had over Karen's reaction would be blown to pieces. In itself, this first rationalization was more than enough.

There was a second, equally compelling justification. It would either be the last or the second last or the third last time with Loretta - one of the last, at any rate. And, after so many secret sessions of lovemaking - crazy, wild, incredible times - one more time hardly amounted to anything. How many Mondays had they met like this? Sixty, maybe? Well, what was the difference, sixty or sixty-one or sixty-two? It certainly wouldn't be enough of an increment to sink him if he wasn't already going down. And abstaining, obviously, wouldn't suddenly make him look like a noble, remorseful hero.

Loretta was wearing a long, white sweater over sexy black tights. Black tights drove Jimmy crazy; she knew they did. He wanted them to be on her and off her at the same time. Loretta pulled her sweater off over her head and waited for Jimmy to get his jeans off, watching him intently. Then she stood with her back against the door of the small room. Jimmy was fully erect. He pulled her tights down to her knees and put his right hand between her legs. She was so incredibly warm and sticky. He began to stroke her and put his finger inside her. Loretta held his eyes in hers. She started to tremble and moan. Jimmy continued to stroke her, harder and faster. Her breath quickened and her whole body began to shake violently. She tensed and stiffened and then suddenly relaxed. Jimmy slowly released his hand and fingers. Loretta's smell was intoxicating; on Jimmy's fingers and in the air. He tasted her on his fingers. 'I want you, Jimmy' she said, and moved away from the door. She quickly pulled off her tights and spread them on the floor, along with Jimmy's jeans and his jacket, lying down with her legs spread. Jimmy was on top of her in an instant, inside of her, out of his head; thrusting wildly at her as hard he could. In a few seconds, he came with a muffled cry and then he collapsed into Loretta's arms, breathless.

'Hey, where's your mat?' said Loretta after a few minutes, laughing, as the hard floor began to feel distinctly uncomfortable.

'Oh, jeez. Sorry' said Jimmy, getting up. He looked over at the small desk, where Loretta had placed the pie, right beside the rolled-up mat. 'Hey, how about some pie?'

'You go ahead' said Loretta, getting to her feet and smiling. She gave Jimmy a kiss. 'I've had enough pie the last two days. There's a fork inside the container.'

While Jimmy applied himself to the pie with great purpose, Loretta pulled on her tights and threw her sweater on. 'I'm cold' she said. She pushed a few items to the back of the desk and half-sat on it, watching Jimmy eat.

'This is delicious' Jimmy said. 'Thanks. Loretta. This is really nice of you.'

'You're welcome. I'm glad you like it. There's lots of things I'd love to do for you.'

Loretta's statement hung heavily in the air for a moment. Jimmy decided his best course was not to say anything. He took a last bite of the pumpkin pie, put the lid back on the container, and placed it on the floor to the left of the door.

Loretta picked up on Jimmy's non-response immediately and her tone began to change. 'Cat got your tongue?'

Jimmy could see clearly what was coming. He tried not to sound too evasive. 'Pardon me?'

'A girl tells you she'd love to do things for you and you don't even give her a smile?'

'Sorry. I didn't know I wasn't smiling. My head's still spinning. Wow. That was so good, Loretta. You're amazing. And I'm not talking about the pumpkin pie.'

Loretta ignored the remark entirely. 'Jimmy, I want to ask you something. I hope you thought about what we talked about last week. Did you come up with anything? Did you say anything to Karen? Let her know things maybe weren't going so good?'

Jimmy had carefully prepared his answer to this very question. He sold the lie as well as he could, trying to come off like he'd taken Loretta seriously, while sounding tortured at the same time. 'It's not so easy, Loretta. I mean, it can't sound like it's coming out of nowhere. We did talk a bit, but it was kind of indirect.'

'What did you talk about?'

'I asked her if her life had turned out the way she thought it would.'

Loretta was ticked off at how wimpy and non-committal this sounded. 'And what did she say? Wait, don't tell me. I don't need to know. And then I bet she asked you about your life right? And what did you say?'

Jimmy kept his cool. 'I said I really didn't know how things would go... what marriage would be like after so many years. How your life changes so much, especially when all your time and energy are going into your children. That I was -'

Jimmy may not have fully understood how bringing up children was guaranteed to be a hot trigger for Loretta. She cut him off. Her voice was louder and angrier.

'Jimmy, I don't want to hear how hard your marriage has been; how raising children kills the romance in a marriage... Jeezus H Christ! Everybody's life is hard, Jimmy. Did you say anything that will actually help us change where we're at? Move it along?'

Jimmy laid down a command performance, or at least he thought he did. 'I'm trying' he said, earnestly. 'You have to take it slow. It's not going to happen just like that. Imagine if I just came out and said "I'm not in love with you anymore. I want to split up". What would happen? She'd wonder how that happened all of a sudden. She'd know I was seeing someone. She'd know I must have been cheating on her for a long time. And then what? She'd kick my ass out of the house and I'd have to go to court to see my kids every second weekend. That's not a good outcome, Loretta.'

Loretta wasn't buying it. She thought Jimmy was just evading the situation, unwilling to confront what he had to do, or too afraid to. 'I'm not a frickin' idiot, Jimmy' she said, angrily. 'Sure, you have to start somewhere. Well then, start. She's going to find out anyway. If she doesn't already know. You have to start being honest. Do you want *me* to tell you what to say? Jimmy, the old times are gone. I want a real relationship with you. I've told you that. You can't just keep your safe little world anymore. It's not real, anyway. It's a big lie. Look at us, Jimmy. Look at what happened tonight. We're made for each other. Your kids will be just fine. It happens every day, to everybody. You can split custody. Your wife will get on with her life; she'll be fine too. We'll be together. I'll help you with everything. But you have to start being honest. And stop treating me like I'm some kind of fool. You asked her how she thought her life was going? Come on. That's ridiculous. That's just avoiding it. I don't want to have to pressure you. But she has to find out somehow. How do you want that to happen? We need a plan, Jimmy. I want to be together.'

Jimmy next employed the second part of his communications strategy for the night. What to do when Loretta pinned his ears back and expected him to come up with something? He wouldn't just stand there, looking stupid, while Loretta kept piling it on. He would get Loretta talking about Duane if he could. If that fizzled out, Plan B would be to lie and promise he'd figure out a way to approach Karen. He'd probably need Plan B at some point anyway.

'What about Duane?' said Jimmy. 'How's all this going to affect him? There's a lot of years there.'

94

It was a master stroke on Jimmy's part and the sharp tension in the room was instantly pushed aside. 'Duane?' said Loretta, with a shrug. 'Yah, it'll be a change for him. But you know what? He doesn't even know I'm there when I'm there. It's like two ghosts moving around the house most of the time. It's cold and empty. Sad, but that's the way it is. We haven't slept together in years. We hardly ever do anything. Maybe go to his brother's or watch TV; that's about it. You can't miss what you don't have, Jimmy. Duane'll be fine. All he wants to do is work on his cars and play guitar. He doesn't need me for that. He never did.'

'Are you scared of the way he'll react?'

'Scared? You mean of Duane hitting me or something like that? Beating me up?'

'He's got a hell of a temper, Loretta. I've seen him totally lose it over some pretty small things. And you know how men can be. Maybe he thinks he owns you or something.'

Loretta thought for a moment and softened her tone. 'You know something, Jimmy? Maybe some people think Duane is a rough, scary guy with only half a brain in his head. He'd just as soon fight you as waste his time talking to you. It's not true. He got in a few fights in his younger days, but those days are long gone. He would never lay a finger on me. He's a decent guy and he has his sensitive side too. He's always treated me fair and with respect. I don't love him, but I trust him.'

7 California Reamin'

Thursday, October 12

At 6:25 in the morning, it's difficult to fool anyone very convincingly, especially yourself. But there stood Jimmy Green, half asleep, trying to do exactly that, approvingly staring at himself in the bathroom mirror, his bare feet cold on the slate floor, keeping a world of troubles at bay for the moment. At 54, the bags under his eyes were becoming more prominent and there was a dull leatheriness to his skin tone. His hair was slowly getting thinner and starting to show grey. But what looked back at Jimmy were his winsome blue eyes, his thick, flared sideburns, and his cool, long, shaggy hair. Easy rider, just like he'd always looked. The greying just made his brown hair look a bit lighter, kind of blonde, he thought, looking even better than when he was in his forties. Before jumping into the shower, Jimmy checked himself out in the long narrow mirror on the bathroom door. He gave himself a couple of reassuring pats on the stomach. Hardly any gut. He was still in great shape. No doubt about it; he still had it.

He reached into the shower and turned the water on, letting it warm up for a moment. It was still too cold when he walked in. Karen had been the last to shower; she didn't like it nearly as warm as he did. The temperature shock fully woke him and instantly a hundred different things crowded in on his thoughts. It had been two long, difficult days for Jimmy, trying to prepare himself, trying to get up some steam. He had the counselling appointment at noon the next day. Then he'd tell Karen about Loretta. He thought he'd say "for the past year" when he told Karen how long it had been. It definitely sounded better than "a year and a half'". Other than that, he would try to be honest. Except maybe for a few things he hadn't made up his mind about yet. Like where they went on Monday nights. The supply room at the school would just sound so humiliating and disgusting to Karen. But maybe he'd just have to be straight about that part. It was hard to come up with a decent, believable substitute that would slip in under the radar. Then he'd deal with Karen's reaction. He'd appear genuinely sorry, because he *was* genuinely sorry. He'd tell her he had made a huge mistake. He'd been horribly wrong. It was over now. She and the girls meant everything to him. He was completely committed to making it up to her and making things right. He'd gone to counselling to help him deal with the situation and to help save their marriage. Why did he do it, she'd ask. It was a mistake, he'd answer, it was wrong, he just wasn't thinking. It was weakness; blindness; stupidity. There was no excuse, no matter what you called it. It wasn't because he didn't love her, because he did. He would do anything he could to make it up to her.

Maybe he should have made love to Karen one of the past two nights, he thought, or at least made some kind of physical gesture. Or would that have felt too weird? It had been so long... And then how would it look if he confessed all of a sudden, a few days later, like he intended to? Wouldn't that make it look worse for him - contrived - like he wasn't being genuine? They could get back to that later; he'd make a real effort.

Jimmy kept coming back in his thoughts to what Karen's reaction would be. He'd gotten progressively more and more worried about it. Really, what was the most likely possibility? No matter what he said, no matter how hard he tried to convince her, she'd probably just be crazy-upset, and want him out of the house. Or she'd be totally devastated. Or both.

There was no way Karen knew already, Jimmy thought. She couldn't... He'd been careful. Something would have been said by now.

Then there was Loretta. How would he tell her? What would he say? Make a big speech? "Loretta, I'm sorry, but I'm not doing this anymore. I've made a decision and it's final. This is the last time we're getting together. I told Karen about us and told her it was over. I'm just as responsible as you for everything that's happened, but it's over. I'm sorry." And then what would *she* say? He'd just have to stand there, listen to her, say he was sorry again and then leave. Yah right, he thought. As if she'd be all calm about it... What if she contacted Karen? She probably would. He'd just have to deal with it. Maybe if she went totally nuts, they'd change their phone numbers and email accounts. What about Duane? Fuck. Duane. Whatever Duane said or did, he'd just have to react, that's all. Mostly take it on the chin. Say as little as possible. He should definitely quit the band before Duane found out, if that was possible. What reason would he give? That he couldn't commit to it anymore, couldn't commit the time... Maybe because his wife was starting a course at nights and he had to be home. Something like that... But then, when Duane found out the truth, that would look pretty wimpy. No, he should probably just talk to Duane straight up, own up to it, face him. After he'd told Karen. After a practice... "Hey Duane, can I talk to you for a minute?" Then, whatever. If Duane came at him - hit him - he'd just take it and walk away. Maybe he could tell him in an email, instead. Would that be too cowardly? Maybe it would be better all round... If he quit before Duane found out about him and Loretta, he'd have to think of an excuse for taking his amp home. He could say he was getting a new amp, selling the old one:

"There's a guy coming over to my house to see this amp tomorrow. Hopefully he'll give me a decent price for it." Something like that might work.

The Drones had a practice that night. Jimmy couldn't remember if there was a new song they were supposed to have worked on. He'd have to wing it. No big deal.

Work... He was doing the main hall floor first thing, as soon as he got there today. Then there were the regularly scheduled classrooms the rest of the day.

Jimmy stepped out of the shower, tried to shake some water out of his ears and began to dry himself off. His troubled thoughts were suddenly interrupted by the quarreling voices of his two daughters, in the kitchen. He quickly threw on his bathrobe and went out to see what was going on. Karen was just walking out of the bedroom, toward the bathroom, for her turn at the shower.

'What's going on out here?' Karen said, annoyed, to anyone and everyone.

'Have your shower' said Jimmy, affectionately. 'I'll talk to them.'

Karen gave Jimmy a half-smile as she hurried into the bathroom. Jimmy's eyes followed her. His wife of twenty-two years... She was eight years younger than him, turning 46 this year. She looked as good as ever. She was five foot four, of medium build, with short, straight brown hair, and bright brown eyes. Attractive and fit. And, when it wasn't six-thirty in the morning and her kids weren't fighting, she had a soft, warm voice and an endlessly patient manner. Her work-day started an hour later than Jimmy's, so she drove the kids to school in the mornings. Jimmy picked them up at the end of the day.

Jimmy walked up to the kitchen table, where ten-year-old Kerry and eight-year-old Lisa were still arguing as they ate their cereal. Cheerios were scattered across the floor.

'What is going on here?' Jimmy said to the girls, just sternly enough to get their attention, noticing the mess on the floor. 'Why is there cereal all over the floor?'

'*She* did it' said Lisa, hopeful that her father would believe her, but at the same time, expecting her older sister's word to carry more weight.

'You were pouring cereal into your bowl' said Kerry. 'You spilled it out of the box.'

'*You* grabbed the box' answered Lisa, not giving an inch. 'You tried to take it from me.'

Jimmy guessed that the flare-up had somewhat deeper roots than simply who got their hands on the cereal box. Lisa had just lost a tooth and the tooth-fairy had visited her room the night before, leaving a shiny toonie under her pillow. She had probably been trumpeting the event to her sister, who would have become instantly enflamed with envy.

'Nobody is going to win this argument' said Jimmy, gaining the girls' silence. 'Lisa, will you please get the garbage bin from under the sink. You can hold the bin for Kerry while she picks up the Cheerios and puts them in. Don't forget to put the bin back under the sink, when you've picked them all up. Now come on, you two. Let's get going and then finish your breakfast, okay? I don't want to hear any more arguing. I have to get dressed and get to work. And you guys have to get ready for school.'

It seemed like a reasonable solution to Lisa, who quickly followed her father's direction. Her older sister Kerry complied but was somewhat less magnanimous, glaring at her as she threw the cereal into the bin.

A few minutes later, Jimmy made his way through the kitchen again, giving each of the girls a kiss and yelling a word out to Karen, who was still in the bathroom. 'Bye. See you later. I've got practice tonight.'

That night, as Jimmy backed his jeep out of the driveway into the lane, he glanced up at the roof of their bungalow. Shingles were starting to curl here and there. The roof had to be redone soon. It had been almost twenty years since he'd put new shingles on. Twenty-one years they'd lived there, he and Karen. They'd put a lot into the place. He shook his head anxiously. Things were going to work out, he said to himself. They had to.

Of all the band members, Jimmy lived closest to their practice facility. Just a mile west on Fleet to Lindsay and then over to Corydon and he was there. On the short drive over, his thoughts turned to how he was going to deal with the band. Maybe he should quit the band right now, tonight, he thought, uneasily imagining Duane's reaction as well as the rest of the band. He was reasonably content with the lie he'd decided to tell: Karen had a night course coming up, one that ran for several months. He was sorry but he'd had little warning. It was something very important to her job and her career and he needed to support her. It was a pretty good story.

The band had a gig coming up, in two days, on Saturday night. He could tell the band that he'd play the gig and that would be his last time with them.

Then he thought again about the way it would look to Duane when Duane found out the real reason. But so what? That would be the least of his problems. Still, he was unsure whether it was the right thing to do or the right time. Maybe he should wait until after the gig and then tell them. Then he could just pack up his equipment and bring it home for good.

Jimmy was anything but sure of himself when he arrived at the former yoga studio. He knew how hard it was going to be to lie to Duane. He was going to have to face him someday, anyway. Maybe, instead of lying, he should just pick a time to tell Duane the truth.

101

Duane, Elliot Munroe and Norman Jones were already there when Jimmy walked in, at 6:55, with his shades on, carrying his guitar. Duane was seated on a stool, with his Stratocaster, playing quietly to himself. Elliot and Jones were sitting on chairs at the other end of the rehearsal area. 'Hey guys' Jimmy said. He laid his guitar case down in front of his amp and took a few steps toward Elliot and Jones, in search of a cord. Finding one on top of Dave Candon's amp, he began to unwind it. Elliot and Jones were in the middle of an animated conversation about songs they wanted to do, and the memorable bands that had recorded them.

'Some of those bands were so short-lived' Elliot was saying to Jones. 'Even with a lot of big-time talent in them. Like Buffalo Springfield... The Flying Burrito Brothers...'

Even though Elliot hadn't even born until 1972, he knew more about music from the sixties and seventies than almost anybody. 'Yah' said Jones. 'Neil Young and Stephen Stills were in Buffalo Springfield, right? I've never listened to the Burrito Brothers. Heard of them, though.'

'They had Chris Hillman and Gram Parsons, from the Byrds' said Elliot, 'and Bernie Leadon, who was one of the original Eagles. But somehow, they just fizzled. Nothing happened for them. Too much drugs, probably.'

'Some of those bands went more in a folk direction' answered Jones. 'Neil Young did a lot of folkier stuff for a while, didn't he?'

Elliot looked over at Jimmy, who was listening in, and gave him a thumbs-up. 'My dad saw Buffalo Springfield, The Byrds and The Mamas and The Papas on the same bill back in the day' Elliot said.

'Wow!' said Jones. 'Have you ever done folk in a band?'

'Not a whole lot' Elliot answered, and then thought for a moment. 'One band, we did a few folk songs. We had a female vocalist who sang great harmony.'

Just then, Dave Candon walked through the door, only six minutes late.

'What the hell, Cans?' said Jones. 'Are you sure you're in the right place?'

'Howdy, boys' Cans replied, walking up to his amp and taking out his bass guitar. 'How're things?'

'Okay, let's get going' said Duane, as both Jimmy and Cans turned their amps on and plugged in. 'Why don't we run through the Kinks medley to get started? Remember there's three "all day and all of the nights" at the end of the first and last verses, but only two going into the solo in the middle. We always seem to miss that.'

As Cans and Jimmy took a minute to tune, Jones tested his microphone. After his conversation with Elliot, he apparently had The Mamas and The Papas on his mind. 'Tasting 1-2-3' said Jones, taking on a lower and deeper voice, and breaking into a mock-up of a front man. 'For our first song tonight, we'd like to do a much-loved song by The Mamas and the Papas. We're going to do the lesser-known, original version of *California Reamin'*. This song tells the story of John and Michelle Phillips, in their early days, when they were madly in love and first moved out to Los Angeles. They didn't have much money and they used to eat in run-down greasy spoons and cheap burger joints. One night, they both ate some bad food and got food poisoning. They both had really bad diarrhea for a spell. That's where the song came from.'

Following his informative introduction, Jones burst into song, doing his best to sound like John Phillips: 'All the sheets are brown.'

With little choice in the matter, the others had been listening impatiently, a captive audience, willing only to allow Jones a minute or so, not quite able to predict the course of his latest silliness.

Jimmy chuckled. Duane shook his head. Elliot surrendered a quick laugh, fidgeted in his seat and adjusted his glasses on the bridge of his nose.

'That's why drummers should never be given microphones' said Cans, with a laugh.

For Jimmy, preoccupied as he was, Jones' typically bad joke served to ease his internal tension a little. Jimmy had more or less decided he was not going to announce his imminent departure from the band. Any remaining uncertainty on the matter was soon swept away completely.

As soon as Jones had gleefully finished his Mamas and Papas performance, Elliot held his hand up, signalling to the others to wait for a second. Duane was just about to roar into the intro to *All Day And All Of The Night*. 'Can we hold on, just for a sec' Elliot said. 'Sorry. I've got something I have to tell everybody.' He was evidently a little nervous, not really making eye contact with anyone, adjusting his glasses. 'I've applied for a new position. It's in Brandon. I interviewed this week. They said they'll get back to me in a week. There's a good chance they're going to make me an offer. It would be a pretty good deal; a little more money and a chance to be a senior partner. It's a smaller firm than the one I'm in now. They do pension and income accounting for a couple of large unions out there. Obviously I'd be leaving the band if I get the job. So I just wanted to give everybody a heads-up.'

For a moment, there was dead silence in the room. All of the other four band members were stunned. Especially Jimmy, who, moments earlier, had been contemplating a very similar kind of announcement.

'How soon would you be leaving?' asked Duane.

'I'd be starting pretty soon. Probably a week or so after they offered me the position.'

'Okay. So you're in for the two gigs we have over the next week and a half?'

'Yah, for sure.'

After the awkwardness of the moment had faded, Dave Candon was the first to offer a word of encouragement. 'Hey, I hope it works out for you, Elliot. Brandon's a nice little town. Be great for your kids.'

'Thanks Cans. I appreciate it.'

Jones, too, offered a friendly word. 'I'm going to miss you, Elliot. You're the only person that ever laughs at my jokes.'

Pretty good timing, Jimmy thought. It almost looked like Elliot and Jones had coordinated the announcement. Jimmy admired Elliot's artful directness. He was a hundred percent sure Elliot already had the job in his pocket. It was just a calculated way of breaking the news, Jimmy thought; probably the best way to minimize Duane's reaction. If Elliot was ready to move out there to work in a couple of weeks, he must have already checked out a place to live. Jimmy thought about his own bogus story, about Karen's night course. How believable would *he* sound? Well, Elliot was leaving and then he was leaving. They'd joined at the same time and they were leaving at the same time... Duane will probably be on BandMix lining up new auditions as soon as he gets home, Jimmy thought. Good thing he decided not to tell the band tonight that *he* was quitting. That's going to go over like a lead balloon now...

'Thanks for the heads-up' Jimmy said to Elliot, wanting to sound genuinely appreciative. 'Good luck.'

'Thanks, Jimmy.'

Jimmy remembered the conversation he and Elliot had had at the last practice, when Elliot told him about his kids. Moving out of town had to make things even more complicated for him.

There was no better way to get past the awkward moment than to play.

'Okay. Everybody ready?' said Duane. Not needing any answer, he ripped off the fabulous chord sequence to start the song. Jones brought the others in with a rim shot and they were off. Elliot sounded fantastic, giving it all he had: 'I'm not content to be with you in the day-time...'

The band began to run through their songs for the upcoming gig. All the songs were tight with only a few small glitches: Jones missed the ending for *Tell Her No* and Elliot forgot to cue the outro for *In The Midnight Hour*. Near the end of the practice, Jimmy found out there was indeed a new song on the slate, - *How Do You Do It*. He hadn't even listened to the song over the previous week, but he thought he remembered it well enough to get through it.

'Can you remind me what the chords are?' Jimmy said to Duane, hoping his lack of preparation wouldn't be too obvious.

'G, E minor, A minor and D' answered Duane.

Jimmy had no trouble until the bridge, where he went to C instead of A minor. Duane signalled for the band to stop, and they tried it again. Jimmy made a different mistake the second time and the band stopped again.

'Jeez, Jimmy' said Duane, annoyed. 'Did you practise this song?'

Jimmy had little choice but to come clean. 'I have to be honest, Duane' he said. 'I didn't have a chance to even listen to it all week. I was just too busy.'

Whether Duane was transferring his frustration over Elliot's announcement or just being his usual ornery self, he was not pleased. 'Come on, that's bullshit' he said to Jimmy, in an angry tone. 'Everybody's busy. We all have frickin' lives. Everybody's gotta keep up his end, Jimmy. Come prepared.'

Though he was a little embarrassed, Jimmy took the admonishment in stride. After three more songs, the practice ended. Duane reminded everyone about the Saturday gig - when they would meet to load the equipment and what time they had to be there.

Predictably, Elliot was the first to leave and the others hung back to talk about replacing him. Duane's displeasure dominated the conversation. Dave Candon and Norm Jones tried to sound upbeat and inject a little humour into the situation. Jimmy hardly said a word.

'It would have been nice to have a little more notice' said Duane. 'I mean, he didn't just find out about this tonight.'

'He's probably been waiting to hear back' said Jones. 'He's not going to say anything to us until he knows what's happening.'

'Remember the insane cast of characters we auditioned before we found Elliot?' said Cans. 'That was something else.'

At the time the band was seeking a replacement for Greg Mazur, Jimmy wasn't yet in the band, so most of what he was hearing was new to him.

'Remember the young kid, the nervous kid? With the Mohawk?' said Jones, with a chuckle.

Even Duane laughed at the recollection. A young man, in his early twenties, had answered the band's ad on Kijiji. In an email, he had assured the band that, despite his age, he loved sixties music and knew a lot of the band's songs already. Duane gave him a list of five songs to prepare and scheduled an audition three days later. The day of the audition, the kid was right on time. When he walked into the room, he was wearing a black wool touque and he was clearly very nervous. When he pulled off the touque, he revealed a truly impressive hairdo: a four-inch-high blue Mohawk, with the rest of his head shaved bald. His first attempt to sing was a disaster. He forgot the lyrics and simply couldn't continue. They tried to calm him down a little and just chat for a while. The young man was pleasant enough but described a world of major troubles weighing on him: he'd lost his job, lost his drivers' licence, had no money and was living temporarily with a friend. The three band members tried to be sympathetic and encouraging. They tried another song. It was worse than the first one. After the kid had come in at the wrong place and missed a few lines, they called it quits. He offered an excruciating apology, pulled his touque back on, over the blue Mohawk, and walked off into the night.

'That hairdo was something else' said Duane, with a laugh. 'I remember thinking, as soon as I saw him - before he even said a word - that this was not going to turn out well.'

'Then there was the guy with the booze' Cans chipped in. 'Remember him? Robert. An hour late. Remember he brought a small nylon case with him? I thought he'd brought his own mike or something. It was full of booze. He had to stop after two songs and have a drink. He was over the top. Remember how he overdid it, to impress us? He had kind of a fake accent, Irish, I think.'

'Yah' said Jones. 'We couldn't get him to leave. He started singing Joe Cocker songs. He was kind of scary. I was the one who had to call him up and tell him we'd picked somebody else.'

'How about that soul singer? Dana.' said Duane. 'Or was that before Greg?'

'Oh yah. Dana!' said Jones, the name jogging his memory. 'I thought he was a woman. All he'd sent me was audio clips. No pictures, no video. I remember telling you guys it was a woman. I had to work on you to convince you to give it a shot, because it was a woman. Then this dude shows up, with the high, soul-music voice. He sounded like Diana

Ross. That was funny. And then he kept emailing me for months after. He *did* have a great voice.'

'How about the short guy, with the big gut on him?' said Cans. 'What was his name?'

'Les' said Jones. 'He could play guitar pretty well, I remember, so Duane wasn't totally against him. But his whole scene was country music. And he was way too fat and ugly to be a front man, anyway. His voice was kind of nasal, I thought. I think he was the first guy we auditioned.'

Cans laughed. 'There's nothing like a serious round of auditions' he said. Then he turned to Duane, who was growing less and less amused. 'It'll be a good time, Duane. We'll find somebody.'

'It's a lot of time and energy' Duane answered, in a sullen voice. 'Especially trying to find guys that are even worth auditioning. Some guys won't even send you audio samples until you've gone back and forth ten times with text messages. I want some help on this, from all three of you. I'll put the notice up on Bandmix and Kijiji, but I want everybody to check out the replies. Okay, we meet here Saturday at 4pm to load the equipment and take it over.'

8 Jimmy Goes To Counselling

Friday, October 13

It was a cool, sunny fall day. And though Jimmy Green *did* carry a mild aversion to the number thirteen, to him, the fact that it was Friday the thirteenth signalled no perilous portent. Whether any particular Friday happened to fall on the thirteenth day of the month, Jimmy took to be an irrelevant coincidence. But matters *other* than the date did trouble Jimmy that day, as he weathered the long drive to his counselling appointment.

Jimmy's destination was a newly constructed health and fitness centre, a flat, square, cheerless building, situated in a cement desert adjacent to the Southwood Mall in Fort Garry. Plodding along in the traffic on Route 90, Jimmy's anxious mind was in full gear. Maybe he should cancel the appointment, he thought. He still could if he wanted to. What good was it going to do? Didn't it make just as much sense to simply tell Karen? Then he started to imagine again how he would approach that dreaded conversation. Exactly what would he say? How much would he tell her about Loretta and him? One minute he felt reasonably confident that he could pull it off. That he could sound genuinely remorseful and convincingly appeal to Karen to keep their marriage and family together. The next minute, he was sure it was hopeless; she would want to leave him, no matter what he said. The more he thought about it, the more problematic it seemed.

He had hardly thought at all about what he would actually say to the counsellor. The original idea - that his seeking counselling would bolster his appeal to Karen - still made sense to him. Now he caught himself thinking that maybe the counsellor might even help him a little; help him figure out what to say, how to start the conversation with Karen in the best possible way. No, that's ridiculous, he immediately countered to himself. All they do is blow a bunch of terms at you, to try to mess you up, to keep you coming back.

Jimmy was almost at the point of turning back when he turned off Bishop Grandin onto Pembina Highway, with the forbidding, drab mall in sight. In another minute, he pulled into the parking area beside the clinic.

Tucking his sunglasses away in the top pocket of his denim jacket, Jimmy squinted up at the sky and walked up to the clinic doors. As the signage indicated, the facility featured an extensive array of services. In addition to family physicians and a number of medical specialists, the centre offered acupuncture, cosmetic surgery, laser eye surgery and fertility treatments, as well as diagnostic labs and several types of counselling. Walking into the cavernous entrance and reception area, Jimmy looked about. Bland-coloured modular furniture lined the walls, surrounding a central administrative area, a series of indistinguishable desks and indistinguishable people behind long counters, all staring at laptops, one after another. It was a busy place, with most seats occupied and people coming and going. Large, leafy plants in ceramic pots were symmetrically placed all around. Sixty-inch high definition TV monitors also caught Jimmy's eye, all with the sound muted; suspended from the ceiling on either side of the administrative area, and all tuned to CNN. It took him a moment to spot a small sign indicating the registration desk.

After speaking to the receptionist, a friendly young woman with blue and silver streaks in her hair, Jimmy slipped into an unoccupied seat between two middle-aged women. Glancing at the other people waiting - the 'clients' as the receptionist had referred to them - Jimmy could only see a few people who were not glued to their smart phones. Most were female, representing a broad spectrum of the population: from African-Canadian women in hijabs, with children in tow, to teenage Caucasians with their piercings, tattoos and gaudy hairdos.

Expecting to wait for ten or fifteen minutes, Jimmy began to mindlessly stare up at the closest TV. North Korea and its proudly displayed missile-launches were the dominant news images. The chubby little psycho president and his psycho haircut were shown prominently, over and over again. Jimmy had his own ideas about North Korea and their missiles and nuclear bombs. He believed that the Americans had sold them most of the technology involved, as well as a vast number of their weapons. Probably through third parties. All those weapons-manufacturing-plants down in Texas had to be kept humming. The American military - not to mention their own psycho president - were just as much a threat to the world as anyone else, Jimmy thought. So why bother getting all worked up about it? There was nothing ordinary Canadians could say or do that made any difference anyway. Looking around the waiting area again, with all the faces trained on their phones, Jimmy thought it would be a relatively easy matter to take over North America. With no weapons at all. You just needed to have enough people, in ordinary civilian clothes. They could calmly walk into the cities and simply take them over. People wouldn't even pay any attention; they'd all be buried in their phones, looking at a never-ending flow of dumb photos and text messages.

After Jimmy heard his name called, a white-jacketed woman appeared out of nowhere and smartly led him down a series of brightly-lit hallways. The woman indicated an office door to Jimmy and instructed him to walk in.

As Jimmy walked into the small office, Dr. Sylvia Wennapulko, the counsellor to whom he'd been directed, rose to greet him. After Dr. Wennapulko introduced herself, she gestured for Jimmy to sit down. Then she closed the door and sat down herself. Jimmy sat down on the only available chair, a black leather chair, facing the counsellor's clean and orderly white desk. The office was windowless, with bookshelves lining the walls on two sides.

'Um, are you a psychiatrist?' asked Jimmy. 'Or a regular doctor?'

'A psychologist' answered Dr. Wennapulko. 'I have a doctorate in Psychology and I'm certified in family counselling.'

Dr. Wennapulko glanced at the open laptop to her right. 'Mr. Green' she said in a warm, welcoming voice. 'I'm just looking over the form I was sent. I see you're married with two children and employed by the St. James School Division.'

'Yes' said Jimmy, trying to settle into a comfortable position in the leather chair.

'Well, I'm afraid that's all I know about you. Can you please fill me in on the nature of your visit?'

'This is all... like... confidential, right?' said Jimmy.

'Of course' said Dr. Wennapulko.

Dressed in ordinary civilian clothes - a patterned button-up shirt and black slacks - Dr. Wennapulko had shoulder-length, wavy brown hair and was wearing dark-rimmed glasses. She was middle-aged and, to Jimmy's relief, had a quiet and unassuming manner. He didn't feel nearly as nervous or defensive as he'd thought he would.

The words unevenly tumbled out of Jimmy's mouth. 'Um, I've been having an affair. I decided to end it and tell my wife about it. It was a big mistake. I really want to save my

113

marriage. I'm not sure how to tell my wife about it. That's about the whole story.'

'I see' said Dr. Wennapulko, in a quiet voice. 'Do you mind if I ask you about the circumstances?'

'Not at all, Doctor Winna-' said Jimmy, trying to be polite, but still a bit nervous and not remembering the last name.

'Please call me Sylvia' the counsellor answered with a smile. 'My last name usually gives people a bit of trouble. Good. Okay, can you tell me about the affair? How long it's been going on, the circumstances... and so on. Anything you feel is important. Perhaps you can talk about why you've had the affair, if you can, in relation to your marriage.'

For the entire time Jimmy had been seeing Loretta, he hadn't spoken a single word about the affair to anyone. Now, as a result of the psychologist's calming manner and weeks of rising anxiety, once he started talking, he found he couldn't stop.

'I guess it's been over a year now. I'm in a band with Loretta's husband. Loretta's the woman I've had the affair with. That's how I met her. It was all about sex. That's what it was supposed to be from the beginning, what we both agreed to. But Loretta - I guess she changed. In the last few months, she's been threatening me and pressuring me, wanting me to leave my wife and be with her. I've never wanted anything like that to happen. It has to end. So I've decided to tell my wife about it and hopefully I can keep my marriage together.'

'If I understand you correctly, Mr. Green, you haven't told your wife about the affair yet?'

'That's correct. But I intend to. I'm very worried about how she'll react. I haven't exactly figured out how to tell her. That's kind of why I'm here.'

'I see. And, just to clarify, have you told the other woman _'

'Loretta.'

'Loretta. Have you told Loretta that it's over with her?'

'Um, no I haven't. I'm waiting until I've told my wife. I want my wife to hear it from *me*. If I told Loretta it was over, she'd probably call my wife and try and blow things up.'

'I see. All right. I can certainly appreciate your tactical challenges, if I might call them that. Before we talk about that any further, I think it would be useful for me to learn a little more about how things have gotten to this point. And how you see your role in the affair; how you see your marriage.'

'Like I said Doctor - Sylvia - things were going fine with Loretta, for a long time. We'd meet once a week and have amazing sex and that would be it. We weren't involved in each other's lives in any way other than that. Everything was fine. My home life was fine; the same way it had been before I got involved with Loretta. I was getting along with my wife the same way as before; my kids were doing great. Everything was getting done around the house. Loretta was happy with the situation and so was I. Then she decided she wanted more; she wanted a real relationship; to be together. And she started pressuring me and threatening me because I didn't. I just never saw it coming, I guess. And now my marriage, my family - everything - could just fall apart.'

'It's certainly not surprising that the situation, the affair, has put your marriage and your home life at risk. Do you share the responsibility for that happening or is it mostly on Loretta? It's definitely a positive step that you've decided to confront the situation now. But your description sounds like you feel you shouldn't *have to*, that things could just as well have continued, as long as Loretta didn't tell anyone or rock the boat. As long as your wife never found out, there would be no need for anything to happen on your part. Is that correct, or am I misinterpreting what you've said?'

'It was just supposed to be about sex. That's what the understanding was. Just sex. We were never going to get involved in each other's lives in any other way, just enjoy the times we got together for sex.'

'I understand. Let me ask you a slightly different question. Have you always believed that the affair - even if it was only about sex - didn't constitute any fundamental betrayal of your wife, that it wasn't potentially destructive to your marriage and family?'

'Yes I did. That's how things were and that's how things would have remained, if it just stayed separate. The rest of my life - my commitment to my wife and my family - would have been the same as before; just as good as before. That's how it's been. I really didn't think anything was at risk or that I was being a bad person. Because it was completely separate, and because Karen - my wife - wasn't going to find out about it.'

'All right. So you're saying that you haven't been giving less to your wife and your family because of the affair?'

'Definitely not. Maybe it's made me a better person to Karen and my kids, because I'm happier in another way that I couldn't otherwise be.'

'Because of the amazing sex?'

'Yes.'

'Would you say then that you can't have a sufficiently satisfying sexual relationship with your wife? Or find a way to sufficiently satisfy yourself sexually without having an affair?'

'Not to the level I do with Loretta. I mean, come on, Doc. You can't have that level of intensity with someone you've been married to for twenty years. It's impossible. Time makes people grow colder to each other in some ways. How long is sex really good between two married people?

Maybe a year? Everybody knows that. I still have sex with Karen sometimes, just like I did before I ever started up with Loretta. But it's not like sex with Loretta.'

'I understand what you're saying. But is it possible to have *enough* sexuality in a marital relationship? Maybe one can't experience a continuing stream of high intensity and passion. But maybe one can still be content. This is an issue all people in relationships have to deal with. To many people, the potential destruction that an affair can bring, is enough of an impediment to stop it ever happening. I'm sure you've thought about this before - what would have happened if your wife had found out about the affair?'

'Yes, but the point is she wasn't ever going to find out.'

'So you thought... but if she had?'

'I wouldn't have done it if I thought she might ever find out. Loretta and I made a deal. It was just something separate, something that had nothing to do with my wife; something that wasn't going to affect anything else. It was something that was just for me; something I wanted; something that I felt I needed. It wasn't going to hurt anybody else or change anything that was already going good.'

'Okay. Let me try and understand this from another perspective. Have you always had this attitude about extramarital sex? That it was all right to 'cheat' - as people call it - as long as the other person never found out?'

'Yes, I have. It's something that has nothing to do with the rest of my life. It's like, in a different compartment. Anyway, if people could just see sex as *sex*, it wouldn't have to be such a big deal. Maybe it's a difference between men and women. Maybe a man can just have sex with a woman and really enjoy it and just leave at that - no other commitment or other things have to be going on. It's just a physical thing that two people can mutually enjoy. Have a good time and then go home. And not have any other expectation or hold or claim on the other person. Maybe women can't do that or can't see it that way. I thought Loretta could. She told me she could, but then she changed her mind, or something changed.'

'So you can have an ongoing, intense sexual relationship with a woman, and have essentially no connection with her, not genuinely care about her, in any significant way beyond sex?'

'Absolutely.'

'And you suggest that men in general may all have this same disposition?'

'Maybe. I don't know. It's possible.'

'We were talking earlier about not being able to have the same kind of satisfying sex with someone you've been with for a long time. So, does the passion and intensity result simply because it's with a new person, someone fresh? Does that constitute the whole allure?'

'Kind of, I guess. But it's *how* the sex is with Loretta, not just that she's new. Not that we do weird, kinky things, but it's the total experience of it; the way she talks during sex, how she moves, the feel of her body; what she likes me to do to her. How she has such amazing orgasms...'

'Okay. But those are things you obviously must have discovered *after* you got involved with Loretta; not before. Logically, they couldn't have been the *cause* of your jumping into an affair with her. Okay, let's just put the quality and nature of the sex aside for a moment. You've said that having the affair didn't have to do with any other involvement with that person - Loretta - and that none was desired or attempted from the beginning. So how can we understand the role of the individual here - Loretta? There are lots of attractive people out there, lots of *very* attractive people out there; very sexy women. Could you potentially have satisfying sex with any one of them, picked at random?'

Jimmy laughed a short, quiet laugh. 'Any one of them? Hmm, I don't know about that. Maybe, if I was in the right state of mind, feeling kind of lusty, and the circumstances were right.'

'So you could potentially have satisfying sex with any woman at all who's reasonably attractive - physically attractive? At the right time, given the right circumstances. No questions asked, no strings attached.'

'I guess. Maybe. I've heard about guys that hook up with random partners all the time. Apparently a lot of guys are like that. One guy I know went on the internet and arranged to meet a woman, a total stranger, for a weekend in Thunder Bay, just to have sex, no strings attached. He said it was fantastic. And he's still with his wife.'

'Has he ever seen the woman again?'

'I don't know. I don't think so. He's not that good a friend of mine; I haven't talked to him in a while.'

'May I ask you about your past sexual behaviour? Have you ever done this before? Had sex with another woman during your marriage?'

'No, I haven't. But I've certainly fantasized about it. Many times.'

'When you thought about it, did you think you'd actually do it if the situation was right?'

'Um, I don't know if I was actually waiting for the day to come or anything. But I've kind of fantasized about a lot of women over the years. Just fantasies; nothing happened.'

'When you had those fantasies, did you ever think that if the opportunity actually presented itself, and if your wife could be kept completely unaware, it would be all right to do?'

'I guess I did, yah.'

'May I ask how long you've had these fantasies? Or are they better thought of as urges, or desires...?'

'They're definitely a kind of desire, that's for sure. I guess I've kind of had them all my life.'

'Have they usually been directed toward women you know, that you run across in the ordinary course of your life? Like Loretta apparently was? Or are they directed at women that have no connection to you?'

'Both, I guess.'

'You say you've had these sorts of fantasies all your life. How long have you been married, did you say?'

'Twenty-two years.'

'Can you describe any particular fantasies you've had over those twenty-two years, any particular women they've been directed to? Other than Loretta, I mean. You don't have to name people, of course.'

'One sticks out in my mind because it was the first place of our own that we lived in - Karen and I. It was six months or so after we got married. We'd been living at her mom and dad's. There was this woman, this couple that lived in the apartment right above us. We'd hear them at night, going at it. It sounded so amazing; like they were just about tearing each other's flesh off. Karen and I kind of laughed about it. We were having lots of pretty good sex ourselves right around then. After a while I started to wonder who that woman was, what she looked like. And how bad she must want it. And how incredible it might be to... to ... you know... to have sex with her. One day I sneaked up to her floor, one floor up, and waited until someone came out of that apartment, to try and get a look at her. And I saw her. I did that a few times. I didn't do anything. I didn't follow her or anything. I was never intending to make a move on her, or approach her, but the fantasy kind of went through my mind. It was just a secret little fantasy I had at the time.'

'Are there any other fantasies you can share?'

'Um, I'd have to think about it. Nothing really jumps out in my mind. The odd teacher at school maybe... Our neighbour across the street... Just ordinary people, I guess.'

'Okay. We've still got a bit of time left, Mr. Green. Can we come back to the deception part of this? You've been able to see this as not cheating on your marriage, as not taking away from your relationship with your wife. Perhaps you might explain that to me a little more.'

'It's pretty simple. I mean, it's not like Loretta and I are spending a lot of time together, doing things. We don't go out for dinner; we don't go to movies or comedy clubs or hockey games, like I do with Karen. We just get together once a week for a couple of hours. I put the same energy into my home life as I always did. Being with Loretta doesn't take anything away from what I am and have been with Karen.'

'And as long as your wife didn't know about the affair, there was nothing to feel guilty about; no reason to feel you'd betrayed anything?'

'I always felt it was okay, because I was sure she wouldn't find out. Otherwise I wouldn't have started up with Loretta. And one other thing, to kind of defend myself here. People aren't a hundred percent honest with each other all the time. Couples don't tell each other about every little thing they do or think. Especially if it would upset the other person or cause problems. But they still do things and have their own thoughts about things. Like maybe a guy likes guns and hunting, or going to boxing matches, or maybe he likes betting on sports. Maybe the woman finds those things repulsive. Maybe if he did those things, it could do real damage to their relationship. You hear people say stuff like that all the time: "smoking would be a deal breaker"; "if he killed animals, I couldn't stay with him." So the guy keeps it to himself and just indulges once in a while, not telling the woman anything about it. Maybe he says he's going on

121

a canoe trip when he's actually going moose hunting. Or maybe he smokes pot when he's watching football at his friend's place, and doesn't say anything about it. There's lots of ways to be dishonest. It's just the fact that it's *sex* that people can't handle. I mean, which is worse? One: just having sex with another woman; not spending time with her, not getting involved in any other way. Or two: becoming good friends with a woman, sharing lots of time and experiences with her, but with no sexual component? Are they both betrayals? Isn't the second one worse? Here's an example. Let's say we had a female vocalist in our band. We don't, by the way. Then I'd be sharing all those musical experiences with her, getting together once or twice a week, talking to her during and after practices and gigs, sharing stories about music, about our lives; laughing, having some great times - like everyone does in a band. Is that wrong? Does that take away from my marriage? I think there's a whole lot more between two people in that situation than if they're just fucking. Oh sorry, pardon my French.'

'I see what you saying. Let me ask you one more thing about the dishonesty aspect. How would you feel if you found out that your wife was doing something similar? Should she feel just as justified as you do? What would your reaction be if you happened to find out somehow?'

'I don't know. I'd go nuts probably. But if I *didn't* know and I never did find out, and if it wasn't changing our life together, yah, it would be just the same for her as me.'

'You see your part in the affair as being outside your ordinary, day-to-day life. It's "just sex". Yet it has led to the other person wanting in on the rest of your life; wanting a real relationship with you. How do you put those two things together?'

'Well, it can't continue now, that's all there is to it. I just have to figure out how to tell my wife - and soon. Loretta is so high-strung and hot-tempered at times. She's been pressuring me and threatening me more and more in the past few weeks. One of these days she's going to do something, like call Karen up out of nowhere, or tell her husband; just to blow everything up. She probably thinks if she does that, I'll have no choice but to be with her.'

'May I ask you this? When you realized she couldn't keep the original bargain - that it was going to be just sex, no strings attached - why didn't you end it right then?'

'I don't know. I guess I thought she didn't really mean it, that she'd cool off like she always had before. I'd think that the next time we got together, she would have calmed down and nothing more would be said.'

'So you didn't end it because you thought she didn't mean what she said?'

'Kind of. Or maybe that's what I was hoping, I guess. And I wanted to be with her. I admit it, totally. I mean the sex thing; it's been unreal...'

'But at some point, you realized she was serious, that it was a real threat. And then what?'

'Well, if I'd just decided to end it, I was pretty sure she would freak. I thought she'd tell Karen and probably Duane too, and make sure she blew up my world.'

'I see. You believed your wife would find out. That's why you were trapped, so to speak; why you couldn't end it even if you thought it was the best strategy.'

'Yes. That's why I'm here talking to you. I have to tell my wife. I don't know how much to tell her or what to tell her or how to tell her.'

'I think it's a good thing you've decided to face the situation - whether you believe she's going to find out anyway or not. Obviously it would be better coming from you.'

'Do you have any advice on how I should tell her?'

'All I can suggest is that you be totally honest with yourself. About everything: about your role in the affair, about your wife and family, and about what your commitment to them should mean. That will all come out in what you communicate. Well, Mr. Green, I think our time is up for today. If you'd like to meet again, we can certainly explore the situation further. I would also be very glad to meet you and your wife together, if you feel that would be helpful in the future.'

What do those people get paid for, Jimmy asked himself, driving back to work, thinking of his counsellor; all they do is listen to people talk about their problems. His thoughts turned to the rest of the day and the weekend ahead. It was Friday. They were taking the girls out for pizza and then to a movie. Then the girls had swimming lessons Saturday morning. On Saturday night, The Drones had the gig at the legion. When was the best time to tell Karen?

9 Saturday Night

Saturday, October 14

As far as gigs go - the venue, the crowd, the money, the band's performance - the Saturday night legion gig was mostly forgettable. For starters, the six hundred dollars the band received was on the extreme low end of the scale. As for the Rockwood Legion, it was indistinguishable from scores of other such halls. The venue's main pub area featured a small bar at one end, a shuffleboard table along one wall and a small, raised stage facing a sizable dancing floor. A series of identical round melamine tables filled the rest of the room, with chrome-legged chairs in heavy-duty, industrial-green upholstery at the ready. Engraved wooden plaques and old framed-photographs dotted the walls. Entrance to the special-events banquet room was chained off from the pub area.

Situated on Wilton Street near Grant Avenue, the Rockwood, as locals called it, was only a mile from Jimmy and Karen Green's home on Warsaw Avenue. But until the Saturday gig, Jimmy had never been in the place. Of the five men in the band, only Duane and Jones had played at the venue before.

One feature the Rockwood lacked that other venues had - which was especially disappointing to Dave Candon - was a pool table or two. But Cans quickly got over it. As soon as the band had set up their equipment and had a few free minutes, he happily took five dollars off Duane, Jimmy and Jones in rapid succession at the shuffleboard table.

On Friday and Saturday nights at the Rockwood, a solid cast of regulars kept the drinks coming, while loud, live

125

music poured out onto Wilton Street, where clutches of cigarette smokers came and went. On Saturday the fourteenth, for their modest fee, The Drones played three one-hour sets with twenty-minute breaks in between, from 8 pm to midnight. It was a nearly full house; an older, blue-collar crowd, men and women in their forties and fifties. And while the band wasn't particularly inspired, they methodically reeled off their list of universally popular songs - Beatles, Stones, CCR - to a very appreciative audience. All night long, the dance floor jumped to life with old favourites like *I Saw Her Standing There, Oh Pretty Woman, Bad Moon Rising,* and *Satisfaction*.

Aside from a couple of harmless clods hopping onto the stage to help out with the vocals, and a big, rowdy drunk staggering into the PA- system speaker and tipping it over, The Drones' three-set performance passed with little incident. No damage was done; there were no fights, no blood drawn, no chairs thrown across the floor.

As the band packed their equipment into Duane's truck at the end of the night, the talk was mainly about the slip-ups and mistakes, as it usually was after any gig. For the respective culprits, these recollections were cringe-worthy. For everyone else, they were hilarious. Elliot Munroe had surprised everyone by starting another verse of vocals at the end of *Mustang Sally*, after the rest of the band had distinctly ended the song with an impressive flourish. Duane had played only one verse of solo in *Red House*, instead of his usual two, hanging Elliot out to dry and causing him to miss a line of vocals. Jones had missed the ending to *Honky Tonk Women*, playing on by himself on the drums, thinking that the chorus would be repeated three times rather than two. The band had neatly overcome those testy moments, as bands do, instinctively playing through the mistakes and covering for one another.

While the band's performance may have been pedestrian, the evening was certainly eventful in another way, particularly for the rhythm guitar player, Jimmy Green. This was because both Loretta Selby and Karen Green were on hand to watch their husbands play. A few weeks before, Karen had vaguely mentioned getting a babysitter and coming out, but Jimmy hadn't thought twice about it. In Loretta's case, her appearance took Jimmy completely by surprise. Loretta arrived just as the second set began, and stayed to the bitter end. Karen only watched the first two sets, having agreed to be home by eleven for her babysitter.

In Jimmy's time with The Drones, it was relatively rare for the band members' wives to show up at a gig. And if they did, it was invariably all of them together. For Jimmy, in the middle of the stage, rockin' and rollin' with his red Gibson, it was highly unnerving seeing Loretta and Karen sitting at a nearby table, just the two of them, chatting.

The Drones ended their second set with an abridged version of The Chantays' instrumental, *Pipeline*. Elliot Munroe's chirpy voiceover previewed the final set: 'We're going to take another short break. Get ready for the most obscene song of the sixties when we come back - the song that the FBI investigated: *Louie Louie*.

Hot, sweaty and wired-up, the five band members joined Loretta and Karen at their table, pulling chairs up. Jimmy sat beside Karen and Duane sat beside Loretta. Jimmy had never been so glad to have the entire band at the same table, an ideal cover as he tried to conceal his extreme awkwardness. His heart was pounding. What had Loretta been saying to Karen, he wondered. He exchanged a few inane words with Karen about how the band had sounded. He asked her about the babysitter.

After a round of complimentary drinks was brought to the table, Jimmy tried to calm down. His main concern was to not appear embarrassed or guilt-ridden and, above all, to

127

avoid making eye contact with Loretta, though he heard every word she spoke to Duane and the others. He thought he'd done quite well, until the time came for the band to return to the stage. By then, Karen had said goodbye and left for home. As Jimmy stood up from the table, he could feel Loretta's eyes on him, pulling on him. For a desperate fraction of a second, he glanced over at her. His face instantly flared as he tried to deflect the intense look she was shooting his way. And then he turned and walked toward the stage, alongside his oblivious bandmates.

At the end of the night, as the men carried speakers and amps and drums out the back door, a second encounter with Loretta was even more uncomfortable for Jimmy. Loretta had lingered for a few minutes and was talking to Elliot Munroe. Jimmy made sure he was busy enough that he didn't have to join the conversation. A tall, younger-looking man, who had been sitting at a table near Loretta's, suddenly walked over and approached Loretta. He was three sheets to the wind, and clearly fancied her.

Loretta was standing with her back to the man. 'Hey baby, can I buy you a drink?' the man asked, putting his hand on her shoulder.

Jimmy looked over at the scene and froze. The mild-mannered Elliot Munroe looked more perplexed than anything else, possibly thinking that the man knew Loretta. The inebriated man was thoroughly disgusting and Jimmy's first instinct was to help Loretta; to jump to her defence; to tell the guy to take a hike in no uncertain terms. But he felt handcuffed and embarrassingly conflicted. He didn't want to step in and risk blowing his cover. In the fraction of a second it took for Jimmy's fear and self-interest to hold him back, Loretta fearlessly swept the man's arm off her shoulder with her right hand and turned around to face him. 'Get out of here, mister' she said, loudly. 'I'm busy.'

Just as the words had left Loretta's mouth, Duane walked back into the room. Instantly sizing up the situation, he wasted no time, charging up to the drunk man and forcefully pushing him back. The man, who was more than a head taller than Duane, stumbled backwards and nearly fell over. 'Fuck off or you'll be picking your teeth up off the floor' said Duane, with an angry scowl.

As witness to the altercation, Jimmy felt completely humiliated, exposed to himself as a pathetic, selfish, coward. It would take him the rest of the weekend to shake the feeling.

'Okay, tomorrow afternoon, one o'clock at Corydon' said Duane to the others, once all the equipment had been loaded. 'Make sure you're there. I'm not unloading all the equipment by myself.' Duane walked Loretta to her car and the men went their separate ways.

Karen was asleep by the time Jimmy joined her in bed. He lay awake for hours, replaying the evening in his head. He was going to tell Karen about the affair. As he had done so many times before, he tried to rehearse in his mind some kind of opening he could use, and tried to imagine how she would respond. She - who was lying right beside him, sound asleep.

Agitated and unrested, Jimmy stayed in bed until past ten the next morning, sleeping and waking in fits and starts. He was eventually summoned by his daughters, who knocked loudly on the bedroom door and then burst in. 'Get up daddy, get up' said Lisa, the younger daughter. 'Mommy made apple pancakes; your favourite' said Kerry at the same time, triumphant at communicating the important information before Lisa did.

'Wow! This is tremendous' said Jimmy, joining the girls in the kitchen. 'I *love* apple pancakes!' He smiled at Karen and sat down at the white kitchen table in the sunlight, trying to hold back the guilt, the fear, for just a little longer. As the two girls watched, he used the maple syrup dispenser to write each of their initials on his pancake, L on the left and K on the right.

'It's Patti's birthday today' said Karen, referring to her long-time friend, as she washed and Jimmy dried.

'Oh yah?' said Jimmy, trying not to sound too indifferent.

'She turned fifty and she's been extremely depressed about it lately. I mean big-time. She didn't want a party of any kind. She refused to go out for dinner with her husband. She threatened severe retribution if anyone gave her a present. I tried to plan a small surprise party with her sister Robin, but Robin blew it and Patti figured it out. So we couldn't pull it off. Anyway, I'm going to make a chocolate cake for Patti and take it over tonight, around eight, okay? You've got nothing planned for tonight?'

As he looked at Karen and listened to her, Jimmy knew he was soon going to become the biggest asshole in the world. When was he going to tell her? It couldn't be this afternoon - he had to meet the band and unpack the equipment and get it set up again. It couldn't be tonight either, he thought; Karen would be out at her girlfriend's. It couldn't be in bed, after she got home, that would be just too cold and insensitive. She'd be rattling on about her friend Patti. If he told her then, she'd probably just jump out of bed and spend the night downstairs. He wouldn't have much of a chance to say anything. And then what would it be like in the morning? No. Definitely not tonight. It wasn't going to be tomorrow morning, either. Everyone would be racing around before work. There was no time then. And the girls would be around, so it was impossible. It would have to be tomorrow night at the earliest, Jimmy thought. But tomorrow night was Monday! What was he going to do about Loretta? She'd be expecting to pick him up on Lanark. He had to cancel. Or just not show. And then take it from there and tell Karen.

A cold bolt of fear raced down Jimmy's spine.

10 Two Conversations

Monday, October 16

After bolting down a couple of slices of toast with peanut butter, Jimmy kissed his daughters and yelled goodbye to Karen. It was ten after seven, a cold Monday morning. His phone gave 2 degrees as the temperature, but it felt much colder. Snow was coming, you could feel it. He started up the jeep, turned on the heater and set off for work, taking Cambridge Street to Academy Road. He had a sensible plan; now it was just a matter of making it happen.

Jimmy had decided to call Loretta and cancel their usual Monday night together. He would call around the time Loretta would be sitting outside Johnny La Montina's house, waiting for him to show up. He had invented a good excuse; that his older daughter's class was putting on a play for the kids' families. He would say he had completely forgotten about the event, until his daughter had reminded him. It was very important to her, so he had to attend. Loretta would likely be more than a little put off by the cancellation, given where they'd left things the previous week. She would probably be expecting Jimmy to offer something - to demonstrate how he'd followed through. If she reacted strongly and was unwilling to wait until the following Monday, Jimmy thought he'd offer to meet her during one of his lunch hours, over the rest of the week. Meanwhile, he would have the conversation - the much dreaded conversation - with Karen tonight. He would tell Loretta it was over the next time he spoke to her.

Things didn't quite work out according to plan. It was Loretta who called Jimmy, reaching him at work a little after noon. By itself, this didn't so much take Jimmy by surprise or catch him unprepared. In fact, he had anticipated the possibility of Loretta calling. It simply meant he would cancel their meeting then. Of course, it would be more awkward to talk in the school, especially if Loretta reacted strongly, so he would have to find an appropriate place to take the call, if it came.

But the *substance* of Loretta's call threw Jimmy for a sharp loop.

When the call came, Jimmy had just done the floor of the small school library and he was carefully returning all the tables and chairs to their former positions.

'Hi, Loretta' said Jimmy.

'Hey babe. How are you? How did your week go?' answered Loretta. It was such a hopeful-sounding statement; it made Jimmy feel even worse.

'Hold on a sec' said Jimmy. 'I'm going to go somewhere quiet where I can talk. Hold on.'

Jimmy walked out of the library and down the stairs into the furnace room. 'Hi, Loretta' he said, when he was safely out of anyone's hearing.

'Hi Jimmy. I can't wait to see you tonight. I really need to - '

'I have to cancel. I can't make it tonight' Jimmy said, interrupting Loretta in a quick burst.

'How come? I really need to see you tonight' said Loretta. She not only sounded disappointed; she sounded hurried; alarmed; speaking a little more quickly and a little more quietly than she usually did.

'My daughter's school. Her class is putting on a special presentation. For the families of the kids in the class. I'd forgotten all about it. Sorry. I have to go. It's really important to Kerry.'

133

'I was really counting on seeing you. I have to talk to you.'

'Maybe we can meet over the lunch hour this week sometime?'

'I'm leaving Duane. That's what I wanted to tell you.'

'What?' said Jimmy, totally stunned. 'When did you make *that* decision?'

'It's not like it came out of nowhere, Jimmy. I've been thinking about it for a while. It's no good the way things are. I don't want to live with him anymore. And I don't want to have to lie and sneak around when I see you.'

'Holy Hannah, Loretta' said Jimmy, trying to mute his shock.

'I really need to see you. To talk to you about things. It's kind of scary.'

'When did you tell Duane?'

'Last night. That's why I need to talk to you. Are you sure you can't get away tonight? Just for a few minutes? Please? I really need to talk to you.'

Jimmy had to quickly recalibrate the situation. At first, he thought maybe he should tell Loretta right then that he was out, that it was over between them. He could easily lie and say that he'd already told Karen. But after what Loretta had just told him, he held back. There was a good chance she would fly off the handle. Maybe she'd drive right over to his school and they'd have a big, ugly scene. Maybe she'd go to Karen's workplace and confront her. And then he'd lose what little advantage he had with Karen, for her to hear the story the way he wanted her to hear it. 'Um. Let me think' Jimmy said. 'Okay, maybe for fifteen minutes, before Kerry's school thing. But that's all I can promise, okay? There's a Starbucks on the corner near Johnny La Montina's. Right on the corner. Academy and Lanark. I'll meet you there at 6:45. I have to be at my daughter's school before 7:30.'

It was all happening at once, Jimmy thought, with a grim shudder. All his carefully laid plans didn't amount to a hill of beans. There was no choice in the matter now. He had to tell Loretta where he was at, that night, and then come home and have the conversation with Karen.

When Jimmy walked up to the Academy Road Starbucks, the sun had just gone down. Loretta was already there, sitting at the window at one end, a large coffee in front of her. From the outside sidewalk, Jimmy took a long look at Loretta before she was aware of him. She was wearing an olive-green leather jacket, black slacks and black leather boots. Her long brown hair was tied back. As beautiful as she was, for Jimmy the spell was broken. The woman Jimmy saw could well have been any attractive middle-aged woman, someone he saw by chance when he was passing, having no particular impact, leaving no trace. In a matter of days, Loretta had gone from an incredible, irresistible sexual force, locking Jimmy into a pattern of obsessive lust, to a vexing problem that he had to deal with, someone he hoped to sweep behind him now, with minimal damage all around.

'Hi Jimmy' Loretta said, once he'd joined her at the table. She put her hand on top of his. He instantly drew his hand back and looked around nervously. 'Loretta, please...'

It was an embarrassing moment for both of them, for vastly different reasons. Loretta felt hurt and rejected. Jimmy hoped nobody in the place recognized him. All he had in his mind was what he needed to say to Loretta; how he was going to manage the big mess he was in.

Loretta was the first to speak. She could see that Jimmy was very uncomfortable, so she spoke quickly and quietly. 'I need a few days to figure some things out. To make some plans. I'm going to get my own place. We won't have to meet in that tiny supply room office. It'll take some time to get everything sorted out; money, the house, all that. It's a scary situation. I'm scared -'

'Of Duane?' said Jimmy.

'Not Duane. The situation. Finding a decent place. How I'm going to be able to afford to live. Being on my own. I'm scared that you won't love me, Jimmy, that you'll get tired of me. Have you done anything on your end? Talked to your wife? I could use a little good news.'

'I'm not doing it, Loretta' Jimmy said.

It was a horrible moment, worse than anything Jimmy could have imagined. Loretta's face... She turned pale. The fragile hopefulness in her eyes instantly vanished, replaced first by a pained recognition and then by a look of desperation. 'What do you mean?' she said.

'I'm not going to leave Karen. I never wanted to. I wanted things to stay the way they were. You knew that. I'm sorry, but I -'

Just as quickly, the look on Loretta's face changed again. For a moment at least, her fiery pride returned. 'How do you keep breathing without choking on your frickin' lies, Jimmy?' she said angrily, no longer concerned with propriety, and loud enough for half of the café to hear. 'You think you're just going to go back to your nice little life? No damage done? Oh; sorry, Loretta. You know what you are, Jimmy? You're a snake. And a coward.'

Loretta began to cry, but she quickly composed herself. She stood up and wiped her eyes with the back of her hand. She took a long hard look at Jimmy, grabbed her brown leather handbag, and walked out of the place. Jimmy hung his head and sat alone with his thoughts for a minute, before leaving himself.

Ten minutes earlier, when Jimmy walked into the Starbucks, he was as prepared as he could have been. He

136

had steeled his emotions and made up his mind. The cruel blow he'd delivered to Loretta, the horrible pain he'd witnessed in her eyes - those were unavoidable. There was no other way. Still, it was a deeply haunting image: Loretta, so vulnerable, genuinely hopeful that their relationship would move in a completely opposite direction. But there was nothing he could have done about it. He had to tell her. Did it really make any difference how he'd appeared to her? Saying sorry a million times, or falling to pieces with shame and regret - what good would that have done? She had to handle her own fall-out from this, just like he did.

Jimmy left the café extremely shaken, with his heartbeat racing. Had he always been capable of such cold treachery? The pain he felt was not Loretta's pain. It was the breaking into pieces of his proud, positive self-image. With nowhere to hide from himself.

Maybe he should have told Loretta he was coming clean with Karen, Jimmy thought. Maybe he should have told Loretta he already *had*. But there was no point worrying about that now. Conversation number one was over; done. He was sure he hadn't seen the last of Loretta, but for now, there was no more he could do. He powered his phone off. A much more difficult conversation beckoned, with far more at stake.

For twenty long minutes, Jimmy sat in his jeep, parked on Academy Road, trying to collect himself before driving off. Maybe he was too frazzled to talk to Karen tonight, he thought. Maybe he should wait another day, when he'd calmed down a little more. No. He'd been putting it off for too long. Loretta was certain to contact Karen now, and make a big dramatic scene out of it. It was only a matter of when. He had to talk to Karen now.

He tried to shake his panicky feeling. Even though he'd been anticipating this moment for some time, and trying to rehearse what he was going to say, it was still terrifying. He had absolutely no idea what to expect from Karen. All he could do was hope she would give him a second chance. And not ask too many questions about Loretta.

When Jimmy walked into the house, he yelled out 'Hi guys' like he usually did. He was back earlier than usual for a Monday night, by over two hours. Because he hadn't been sure how long his meeting with Loretta would be, he hadn't said anything to Karen about getting back earlier. He had a perfectly good excuse ready, but he knew it wasn't going to matter very much. He hung up his jean jacket in the landing, pulled off his cowboy boots and walked in. He could hear the water running in the bathroom and the girls' voices. 'Hi guys' he said again, a little more loudly. It was bath-time. Karen poked her head out of the bathroom. 'Hi Jimmy' she said. 'I'm just running Lisa's bath. You're home early?'

'Hi Daddy' yelled Lisa from the bathtub.

'I forgot to tell you it was my last lesson' said Jimmy. 'It wasn't a lesson, really. We just talked a bit.'

'No more lessons?' Karen said, from the bathroom.

'It's time. Probably could have shut it down a while ago' said Jimmy, sounding convincing, even though the lie was half-hearted.

'You should go in and say goodnight to Kerry. She had a bit of a tummy-ache, she said. She's already in bed.'

Jimmy walked into Kerry's room. The light was on and Kerry was sitting up in bed, busy on her kid-proofed iPad. Karen's old iPad. That was an argument Jimmy had lost. Karen had disabled browsing and was convinced it was perfectly fine for Kerry to use. Kerry had promised to share it with her younger sister, who had to wait until she was nine to get her own.

'Hi sweetheart. How's your tummy?' said Jimmy.

'Hi Daddy' said Kerry, barely looking up from her iPad. 'Um, it's better now.'

'That's good. Okay, give me a kiss goodnight. Lights off in half an hour, okay?'

Jimmy walked into the kitchen and poured himself a glass of cranberry juice. He could see that Karen had left Lisa to her bath and was sitting in front of the TV in the living room. After downing the juice, he walked over and sat down beside her on the leather love-seat.

Karen had been binge-watching the last three seasons of *Girls* over the past few weeks. 'You should watch this with me, Jimmy' she said. 'It's a really good series. It's not like *Sex In The City* at all. Really. You'd like it.'

'Um, I don't think so. Thanks for the invite, anyway. Actually, before you get too far into it, I want to talk to you about something. I'll just get Lisa to bed after her bath, okay?'

With the girls snugly in bed, and the video paused, Jimmy finally had a chance to talk to Karen. He again sat down beside her on the love seat.

'This is serious, Karen' said Jimmy. 'All I can do is hope that you'll forgive me.' The way he said it - the fear in his voice, the guilt in his eyes - pretty much eliminated any doubt Karen might have had as to what he was referring to. She was about to speak but she stopped herself.

'I had an affair' said Jimmy. 'It's over. It was a huge mistake. I was just stupid. It will never happen again. Ever. I swear to you. I had to tell you.'

Karen gasped. She put her hand over her mouth. Her face turned pale. 'You had an affair? When?'

'The past year.'

'For how long? How many times did you - '

'For most of the past year. I'm sorry. I'm begging you to forgive me, Karen. I love you. It was wrong. I was wrong. Nothing I say can - '

'For the past year? Where was I when all this was happening?' As Karen spoke, her voice started to rise. She caught herself and lowered it. 'How did you - '

'It was on Monday nights, when I was supposed to be going to guitar lessons.'

'Every Monday night you went out and had sex with another woman?'

'Not every Monday night. A lot of Monday nights.'

'And then you just came home? And acted like nothing had happened? How could you do that, Jimmy?'

Karen started to cry.

'It was horrible of me. I messed up, Karen. I'll do anything to make it up to you.'

'Why, Jimmy? Why? Can you explain that to me? What happened?'

'Nothing happened. It was just a big mistake. It was wrong. I can't explain it in any way that will... It was just a huge, stupid mistake. Whatever word I use would just be a word. I could say I had a mid-life crisis, or I was blind, or I was stupid... I don't know the right word. It was just wrong. I know I was wrong and I want to make it up to you. I'm asking for a second chance. I went to counselling, because I wanted to deal with this in the best way. I wanted to be honest. I was scared. I didn't know what to do or how to tell you. I was so scared to tell you.'

'Who was it, Jimmy? Wait. I don't even know if I want to know. No. I do want to know. Who was it? Is it someone I know?'

'It was Loretta Selby.'

'Loretta Selby? Duane's wife?' A second wave of shock hit Karen. She looked like she'd just seen a ghost.

'Yes.'

Through her tears, Karen struggled to keep her voice down. 'Loretta? God. I just talked to her a few days ago. At the legion. And all the time you and her were... You were fucking Loretta? How could you, Jimmy? How could you?'

Despite her best efforts, Karen's crying increased. Jimmy tried to put his hand on her shoulder, but she threw up her arm and recoiled. 'Don't' she said. 'Please don't. Just leave me alone, please.' She got up and walked across the room and down the basement stairs. Jimmy sat watching her, not knowing what to do. He decided to stay where he was and just wait.

Several minutes later, Karen quietly emerged from the stairway, clutching a ball of tissue. She walked over to Jimmy and stood in front of him. She was bitter, but calm, and she spoke quietly.

'Do you love her, Jimmy?'

'No.'

'Does she love you?'

'No.'

'Why, Jimmy? How could you spend so much time with her if you weren't in love with her?'

'It was just sex. That's all it was. I know that doesn't make it any easier to hear, but... It didn't change anything about how I feel about you or our life together. That's not an excuse. I was wrong. It never should have happened. I just lost my head. I swear to you it will never happen again. I just -'

'Just sex? I thought you didn't even want sex anymore. I stopped trying to initiate anything, because you just didn't seem to be interested. I thought maybe it was just something we were going through, after so many years together. How can you possibly say that? Just sex? As if having sex with someone else wouldn't affect me? My god, Jimmy? Where did you get an idea like that from?'

Jimmy could do nothing but hang his head.

'I just don't get it, Jimmy. Why did you tell me? Why did you decide to tell me? Especially after all this time? If you really believed you were wrong, and you really learned something from it, why say anything? Did she dump you or something? Maybe you panicked? Were you going to run off with her and she changed her mind? And you were all crushed? And now you have to confess? And I'm supposed to tell you it's all right? Let's forget about it and move on. Shit happens...'

Karen walked out of the living room and down the hall into their bedroom, closing the door behind her. Jimmy remained sitting on the love seat. The video was still paused on the monitor in front of him. He turned it off and turned off the light beside him. A few minutes later, Karen returned and again stood in front of him.

'I don't know what to do about this, Jimmy' she said, in the near darkness. 'How can I believe anything you say? I just can't.' She turned to walk away but stopped. 'I do *not* want to talk about this in front of the girls, okay? I do not want them to hear anything about this. Okay?'

Jimmy nodded his head.

Karen started to walk away but again stopped. 'Does Duane know about this, Jimmy?'

'I think so.'

'When was the last time you were with her? When was the last time you -'

'A few weeks ago. I talked to her since then, to tell her it was over.'

Karen turned and walked away and this time, didn't return. Jimmy spent a troubled, sleepless night on the loveseat, half-expecting Loretta to pound on the door at any moment.

11 Leaving The Drones

In the days following Jimmy's upsetting disclosure, Karen and Jimmy awkwardly enacted roles that they had to make up as they went along. Their two daughters were blissfully oblivious of the tense, difficult circumstances hidden from view. In one way, the shaky pretence they maintained enabled Jimmy to cling to a sliver of hope. At least Karen hadn't exploded, and for the moment, she wasn't demanding that he leave. Family life, in its structured, external form, somehow proceeded as usual; meals were prepared, laundry was done, the kids went to school, Jimmy and Karen went to work.

When there *was* a chance for Jimmy and Karen to talk about the situation, they hardly spoke at all. Jimmy thought he should wait for Karen to initiate a conversation, to break the tension. When she didn't, he would hurriedly blurt out a few words, about being sorry, about having been to counselling, about promising never to do it again. Such words seemed to make no difference to Karen. She heard them, but her thoughts were somewhere else. She was detached and unreceptive. She would either just look at Jimmy and say nothing, or say that she didn't know what to do. 'We have to talk about this' Jimmy would say. 'I know' Karen would answer. And they would go back to whatever they'd been doing and not talk. For the first few days, they awkwardly navigated the situation, playing off each other's cues when required. Jimmy's sleeping on the couch was explained away without difficulty.

From Monday to Thursday, as Jimmy staggered his way through the awkward tension, there was one thing that provided a twisted measure of relief: Loretta didn't show up. Not at the Warsaw Avenue house, and not at his workplace or Karen's. Nor did she call. Jimmy had too much to deal with at home to be overly puzzled or worried about it. Even if it was only a temporary reprieve, he was grateful for it. For the moment at least, there was one less calamity to contain.

Next up was facing Duane. Jimmy intended to deal with that at practice on Thursday.

Driving to practice, Jimmy was extremely anxious. His plan was to announce to the band that he was leaving right at the beginning of the practice. Then he would carry his amp, cords and mike stand out to the jeep. But how was that going to go? Duane might confront him as soon as he walked in. He might go psycho. Maybe he'd hit him. Maybe there wouldn't even *be* an opportunity to make his bullshit announcement to the band. In any case, whatever Duane did, or said, Jimmy had made his mind up to just let it happen.

When Jimmy walked into the former yoga studio where The Drones practised, his heart was pounding. Even wearing his trademark sunglasses, he still felt totally exposed, as he wasn't carrying his guitar. Duane, Elliot and Jones were already there. On the surface, it looked like any other practice. Elliot and Jones were off to the side talking. Duane was running through some licks on his Stratocaster, sitting on a stool facing his amp.

'Hey guys' said Jimmy, feeling very nervous, but willing himself on. He stopped just in front of the stage, midway between Duane and the other two men. Duane looked up and nodded. Elliot and Jones said hello. Noticing that Jimmy had no guitar, all three men stopped what they were doing. Jimmy seized the moment, looking first toward Elliot and Jones, then at Duane, and then at a point somewhere in between.

144

'I have to quit the band, guys' said Jimmy, blurting it out abruptly, but doing his best to appear resolved. 'Today. It's personal. There's stuff going on in my personal life. I really don't want to go into it. Sorry to leave you guys in the lurch.'

Taken at face value, Jimmy's announcement, though not identical to Elliot's, came so soon after, that its effect had to be somewhat diminished by comparison. That was certainly how Jimmy had projected the impact, at least in relation to Jones, Cans and Elliot. For what it was worth, it was a sensible analysis, though Cans wasn't even present, and Duane, of course, was another matter entirely.

For a moment, no one spoke. Jones was obviously waiting for Duane to say something. When he didn't, Jones broke the silence. 'Sorry to hear it, Jimmy' he said. 'I hope things work out okay. We'll miss you.'

Jones was genuinely surprised, but it wasn't in his nature to read more into Jimmy's statement. Elliot, on the other hand, couldn't help but think that Jimmy's timing was linked to his own leaving. 'Good luck, Jimmy' said Elliot, walking over to Jimmy and extending his hand. 'It's been a lot of fun playing with you. All the best.'

Duane remained conspicuously silent until Jimmy walked over and unplugged his Marshall amplifier. 'Here, I'll help you with that' said Duane. The Marshall wasn't large in size, but it was quite heavy. Jimmy usually struggled to carry it on his own. Ignoring Jimmy's objections, Duane lifted the heavy amp up from the floor and carried it to the door. Jones walked ahead of him and opened the door. Jimmy followed closely behind with his cords and his microphone stand. 'Thanks, Duane' he said. 'I can manage from here.' 'Don't worry about it' said Duane, continuing out the door to Jimmy's jeep.

'See you guys' said Jimmy to Elliot and Jones, stopping for a moment to shake hands as he walked out the door. 'Keep in touch.'

Jimmy was parked beside the other men's vehicles, forty feet or so from the doorway. When he reached his jeep, Duane was standing near the back of the vehicle, where he had put the amplifier down on the ground. Jimmy set his stand down, along with his cords, and popped open the back of the jeep. As Duane watched, Jimmy hoisted the amplifier into the back of the jeep, and then slid in the cords and stand. 'Thanks for the help, Duane' he said. 'I appreciate it.'

Duane had a peculiar look on his face, one that Jimmy couldn't read. He didn't look particularly angry or threatening, but Jimmy was still very much on edge, expecting Duane to say something or do something at any moment.

'You're a good rhythm player, Jimmy' said Duane, extending his hand. His voice was uncharacteristically quiet, and though he had a grim look on his face, he was anything but angry or out of control.

Surprised and greatly relieved, Jimmy shook Duane's hand. 'Thanks. Duane.'

Duane continued: 'If things turn around for you, give me a call. It's going to take a while to find a vocalist, anyway. I'm thinking of poaching somebody from another band this time.'

'Okay. Hang in there, Duane.'

'Hell yah.'

Jimmy was too stunned by Duane's response to even try to understand it. Driving home, replaying the conversation in his head, he was nearly incredulous. Was it because Elliot and Jones were looking on? No, Jimmy thought, that wouldn't make a bit of difference to Duane.

It just seemed weird.

12 A Plan To Get Away

Jimmy Green's simple mind was awash in troubles and uncertainty. Keeping his head above water took all of his energy; staying painfully alert, saying little, anxiously hoping for a possible opening with Karen. As for Loretta, knowing how strong-willed and emotional she could be, Jimmy had anticipated one and only one kind of response: a furious, vengeful spectacle, bent on the destruction of his marriage. If she was going down, then he was going down too. When one whole day and then another passed, with absolutely no sign of Loretta; no sight, no sound - no explosive confrontation - Jimmy silently thanked his lucky stars. He had no doubt that the storm was coming, but in the meantime, his whole focus was Karen and his children. Maybe, somehow, in the relative calm, Karen would soften a little. Maybe they could begin to talk things out, to try to get over it.

But Loretta's reaction was entirely different. It was one of overwhelming recognition and intense repulsion. Jimmy was so far from where she wished he was, from where she thought he was. She had spent the last several weeks trying to convince him, to pressure him, to goad him. All she'd really managed to do was convince herself. And it was all delusional. How could she have been such an idiot? She was utterly humiliated. She should have listened to what Jimmy had said, what he'd been saying all along. You can't force someone to want you, she explained to herself, to want to be with you. Jimmy's marriage, his safe little life, was a big lie. But pressuring him to give it up, when he didn't really want her? That was ridiculous. All Jimmy wanted was to get laid and to get away with it. It could have been with anyone. She meant nothing to him beyond that.

Still, something constructive had come out of it for Loretta. She had found the will to deal with her bleak, empty marriage. It wasn't that she hated Duane. She just wanted more out of life. It was that simple. And that's what she was going to get. She was going to see it through, on her own.

The conversation she'd had with Duane, that Sunday night, was remarkably short and remarkably subdued. Thinking back on it, Duane's reaction actually made a lot of sense to Loretta. He'd never been easy to shock or set back on his heels. And he rarely showed his feelings. He did have a big temper, but she hadn't provoked him; she hadn't accused him of anything. Her plain, direct tone probably helped too. On the other hand, maybe he wasn't all that unhappy to imagine her gone. Or maybe he didn't think she'd actually go. Maybe he thought she wouldn't be able to manage for very long.

When she'd told Duane, he was sitting in the living room, fiddling around on his Martin, half-watching a hockey game on TV, with the sound off. She walked into the room and sat down on the couch beside him. 'Who's playing?' she said, looking vacantly at the television. Duane stopped playing his guitar. 'Um, the Boston Bruins and Las Vegas' he said. 'Las Vegas has a team?' said Loretta, not at all interested, but trying to edge into what she wanted to tell him. 'Yah, as of this year' answered Duane. He was about to grab the remote to un-mute the sound when Loretta just came out and said it.

'Duane, I have to talk to you. About us. About our marriage. I have to leave. I have to get away. I don't want this life anymore.' She paused for an instant to make sure she had his undivided attention.

148

'I can't do this anymore, Duane. Live here with you. Keep on living the same way. It's not enough for me, Duane. I have to make a change. I've thought about it for a long time. I have to figure some things out, like how it'll all work; getting my own place.'

'What happened all of a sudden?' Duane answered, sounding relatively unperturbed. 'Things have been going pretty good, haven't they? Same as always?'

Even if Duane's tone of voice was matter-of-fact, and didn't betray any fear or alarm, Loretta could see from the look in his eyes that she'd hurt him.

'That's the whole point, Duane. Things *have been* the same. It's not good enough anymore. Maybe it is for you but it's not for me. It hasn't been for a long time. I have to get out of it.'

'You got some other guy?'

'It's got nothing to do with another guy, Duane. I just want more out of life. I have to be on my own.'

'I think that's bullshit, Loretta. You must have another guy.'

'Duane, I want to change my life, okay? I want to travel and do other things. Have my own place. Maybe I *will* find someone else. Maybe *you* will. I just can't go on living my life like I have been. I'm not happy. I haven't been for a long time. I feel like a frickin' zombie, just putting in the miles, day after day after day. It's the only life I've got, Duane. I deserve a chance to be happy.'

'Aren't you being kind of drastic, Loretta? Maybe you should just take a little holiday or something. We've been together more than thirty years. We've done pretty good compared to a lot of people.'

'I've made up my mind, Duane. Look, I know, it must come as a shock, but it's what I have to do. You're a good man. I'm not going to stand here and tell you you got a million faults. That's not true and that's not what this is about. This is about me. What I need out of life.'

'I think you should think about this Loretta. If there's things I can do that I'm not doing maybe we can - '

'Duane, I know you. You know me. We're not going to change. You're not going to change. And neither am I. If we were ever going to live any differently, it would have happened ten or fifteen or twenty years ago.'

'I don't think you ever got over not having kids, Loretta.'

'You're right, Duane. I never did and I never will. That's been built in to our lives for a long time. But I accepted it. And we went on living. But I'm just not happy, Duane. I have to do something about it. While I'm still young enough.'

'I think you should think about it, Loretta.'

'I have thought about it. For a long, long time. I just wanted to tell you. I have to figure out my plans. And don't worry, I'm not expecting you to pay my way.'

'Well that's really nice of you, Loretta' said Duane, sarcastically, showing some frustration and a hint of anger for the only time in the conversation. 'As if that would ever happen.'

To Loretta, it seemed like a good time to end the conversation, at least for the moment. She walked out of the living room and Duane picked up the remote and turned the sound on.

When Jimmy showed his true colours at the Starbucks the following night, coldly rejecting her and humiliating her to the core, Loretta knew exactly what she had to do. She had to leave. She had to get away, at least for a while. Away from all the negative energy in her life. From everything that had turned her into the pathetic, humiliated wreck she saw when she looked in the mirror. Away from lying and deceiving. Away from Jimmy. Away from Duane. She had to see her way through it. Make some plans.

Loretta quickly came up with an idea: her sister Cathy in Calgary. Cathy and her husband Bob owned a condo in Kananaskis Country, in the municipality of Canmore. Cathy had offered the condo to her and Duane before. It was an open invitation, she said. Any time it wasn't being used, she and Duane were welcome to it. They had never taken her up on the offer, not once, over all the years. She had tried to get Duane to go with her a few times, but then given up. Duane had just never liked Bob. He thought Bob looked down on him. Bob was the rich, university-educated orthodontist, with a big, expensive house in Roxboro. He drove fancy new cars and belonged to private clubs. Duane was the uneducated labourer, digging up foundations, fixing up old vehicles, spending his weekends at pubs and legions. Getting together as couples had never been very comfortable. Duane said he would never take any handouts from Bob and that's the way things had remained.

Cathy and Bob mostly used their condo in the winter, when they would go skiing, and maybe for a few weeks in the summer. Chances were pretty good that it was sitting empty for the month of October. So Loretta decided to call Cathy up and check it out. She could drive out there the next day or the day after. It would be the perfect place to get away to, and take a little time to figure things out.

Loretta hadn't spoken to Cathy in more than five months. They were still close, but that's just how things had gone. Time just kept drifting by. It wasn't just that Duane didn't like Bob. They just lived in different worlds. Cathy, with her rich husband and her rich lifestyle, her pampered son Brendon... It was funny how Cathy still acted like the older sister. Like she was so much wiser and so much more experienced; like she still had to protect Loretta and tell her what to do... It was ridiculous. She was only three years older than Loretta. Maybe that was a big deal when Loretta was fifteen, but at fifty-one? And what could Cathy tell anybody about anything? She'd never had to worry about making ends meet. Anything she wanted, she just bought. Still, she lectured to Loretta every time they spoke, advised her, judged her, told her what to do.

Cathy didn't know about Jimmy. After the way she'd put Loretta down about Ian Cooper, Loretta decided she'd keep her private life private, even with Cathy. She didn't want to be preached to again. She didn't want to hear Cathy moralizing about marriage, telling Loretta there was something wrong with her, that she should go to a shrink. As if! That's what celebrities did, and rich people like Cathy; spend thousands of dollars to feel good about themselves. Cathy had been shocked to hear about Loretta's affair with Ian Cooper, and mostly dismissive when Loretta told her how much she looked forward to being with him, how gorgeous he was, how much it raised her spirits to actually want to be with a man again. It was wrong, Cathy had told her. She was making a big mistake. It was horrible to cheat on her husband, to lie to him. If her marriage was dull and lifeless, and wasn't enough for her, she should take steps to improve things. It happened to everybody, Cathy told her. You had to think of ways to make it better. Things *you* could do. Lying and cheating was only going to lead to disaster. It would destroy everything she'd spent a lifetime building. What would Duane do if he found out? Maybe he'd go crazy and beat her up. And maybe he'd be justified. What else could she expect? And what about supporting herself, Cathy asked Loretta. Her pension was way too small to live on. Did she think Duane would give her anything, if he found out she was cheating on him? She'd get nothing of his money, Cathy was sure of that. And she'd have to crawl around in the mud to even get what belonged to her.

Duane's money? Loretta had answered with a laugh. What money? He spent every penny he earned on guitars and cars.

Cathy somehow managed to mention Loretta's pension every time they talked. As if it had been *Cathy's* idea. Loretta was certainly grateful, but it had been *Bob's* idea, not Cathy's. Twelve years before, when Loretta was still working at Sears, Bob convinced Loretta to switch to a defined contribution pension plan. She cashed out her existing plan and Bob invested it for her. Because of that, when Loretta lost her job at Sears, she retained her full pension investment, twenty years of it. Not like a lot of people she knew, who had stayed in the old plan, and who would be lucky now to even get a fraction of their benefits.

Because of Cathy's sermonizing response to Ian Cooper, Loretta had decided not to say anything to Cathy about her love life anymore. There was no point. She didn't need any more lectures about how to live her life. Even though Cathy always asked her, it had been more than two years since she'd told her anything. She hadn't even told Cathy when it ended with Ian, or why. And she'd said nothing at all to her about meeting Jimmy.

Loretta called Cathy on Tuesday morning, October 17, the day after her disastrous meeting with Jimmy in Starbucks. Cathy took the call from her Calgary home.

'Hi Loretta, how the heck are you? It's been a while!'

'It has. How are you? How's Bob?'

'Good, good. We're fine. Brendan's at Simon Fraser, doing a B.A. I'm not sure I told you about it. He seems to have really settled down, so we're really happy about that.'

'Great. Glad to hear it, Cath.'

'How about you? Things going well?'

153

'Um, not exactly. I'm calling to ask you a favour.'

'What's up?'

'I need to get away for a few days. I was wondering if I could stay in your condo in Kananaskis... if you guys aren't using it, of course.'

'What's going on? Are you all right?'

'Uh, things haven't been great between me and Duane. I'm thinking of moving out. Getting my own place. I need to figure some things out; make some plans.'

'Wow. When did all this happen, Loretta?'

'It's been happening for the last thirty years. Things haven't been great for a long time. You know that. I need more out of life. I want to do things. It's never going to happen with Duane. Jeez, I'm over fifty, Cathy. Everyone deserves a chance to be happy, right?'

'Are you still involved with that guitar player, Loretta? What was his name? Cooper, right? Ian Cooper, wasn't it? Is that what this is about?'

'This is about *me*, Cathy. Me and my marriage. I'm trying to make a change in my life, okay?'

'Will you be in the condo alone? I mean, are you -'

'I'll be alone, all right? I just want to get my head together. I'm asking you for a favour.'

'You're welcome to the condo, Loretta. For sure. When would you be coming out here?'

Maybe tomorrow or the day after. Maybe not until the weekend. I have a bit of work to get done. Nothing that urgent, I guess, but... I won't stay more than a week.'

'As long as you want. We won't be out there until the end of December. Maybe later.'

'Great. I really appreciate it, Cath. I'll call you sometime, when I get out there. Is there a key somewhere?'

'I'll call up the condo manager and tell him you're coming. His name's Gary. He lives in the same building.

154

You can get the key from him. I'll call him tonight. Do you know how to get to the place?'

'I still have the directions I wrote down a few years ago. When we were going to make it out there for Bob's fiftieth birthday. It looks pretty straightforward. Canmore Star Mountain, right?'

'That's right. Our condo is 271. Loretta?'

'Yah?'

'How would you support yourself?'

'That's one of the things I have to think about. I've been making a little money with my sewing business. So I'll keep that up. And I'll probably start to draw down my pension. For a while, anyway. I have to figure out a monthly amount and how it's going to affect -'

'Your pension? Loretta, you're only fifty-one! We really worked on that for you. So you'd have something. You can't start taking that money at fifty-one. You'll have nothing left. Jeez, Loretta.'

'I'll do what I have to do, Cathy. It's my money, for heaven's sake. Once I figure out what I'm going to need, I'll have a better idea how much I should take out every month. Don't worry, Cathy. I'm not going to show up at your door with my hand out.'

'I'm not worried about that, Loretta. That's not fair of you to say. I'm worried about *you*. About *you*. Okay?'

'Okay. Sorry. Look, I can take care of myself. I always have. Anyway, it's okay, then? The condo?'

'Definitely. If you want some company, I can join you for a day or two. Just let me know, okay?'

'Thanks. I think I just want to spend some time on my own. But I'll let you know if I change my mind. Oh, and one other thing. I'm not telling Duane where I'm going. I'm just going to say I'm going to be away for a few days. I really don't want him to contact me. I don't think he'd ever come out there after me, but you never know. So if he calls

you, can you please just say you haven't heard from me?
Okay? You haven't heard from me.'

'Will do.'

'Thanks, Cathy. I really appreciate it. And thank Bob too,
okay?'

'I will. Don't forget to bring a parka. And make sure
you've got a windshield scraper. And throw a shovel in
your trunk. Just in case. There's been snow up there
already.'

Loretta decided to leave the next morning, Wednesday.
She would leave Duane a note. That afternoon, she checked
the oil in her SUV and filled it up with gas. Then she made
a trip to the credit union where she and Duane had their
accounts. She withdrew fifteen hundred dollars from the
ATM, intending to use cash for all of her purchases over
the next week. That way, Duane wouldn't be able to track
her through her credit card, which was in both their names.
He would probably guess she'd called Cathy, but Cathy
wouldn't tell him anything.

Next, Loretta made a short trip to the Family Foods store
near their home, on Salter Avenue. She purchased eggs and
cheese, fresh fruit and vegetables, and a case of bottled
water. She would pack the car after Duane left for work the
next morning.

That evening, conversation between Loretta and Duane
was minimal. There was a chilly distance between them,
but it wasn't much different than other days. Neither of
them said anything about their marriage or about Loretta
wanting to leave. Loretta imagined that Duane was waiting
for her to say something, probably believing she was
thinking things over, that things were still very much up in
the air.

As Duane obliviously watched the hockey game in the
living room, Loretta thought about the next day. She was

going to get a late start, so she'd probably only make it to Swift Current. She'd find a cheap motel there and then leave early the next morning. For food, she'd cut up the raw fruit and vegetables. She'd take the block of cheese and half of her homemade corn chowder soup; leave the other half for Duane. And she'd make egg salad sandwiches. She'd better get started. Duane would think she was just preparing food for the rest of the week. She washed and peeled the fruit and vegetables and threw five eggs into a pot on the stove to boil.

There was a lot to do. She was pretty sure Duane wouldn't twig onto what was going on, but she was still a bit nervous. In her haste, she nicked her finger cutting the pineapple, and spilled soup on the counter in transferring it to a smaller container. At one point, Duane walked into the kitchen to grab a can of diet coke from the fridge. He showed little interest or concern, beyond grabbing a carrot stick from the cutting board where Loretta was working.

Loretta decided to make the sandwiches the next morning. She cleaned up the kitchen and took the garbage out for their regular pick-up the next morning. She had already put a small shovel into the back of her SUV, but she had been unable to find a windshield scraper. After wheeling the garbage bins out to the front street, she checked the back seat of Duane's truck. Sure enough, there was a scraper on the floor. Opening and closing the door of the truck as quietly as she could, she grabbed the scraper and put it into her own vehicle.

When she got back in the house, Duane was still watching his hockey game.

What else? She would remember to throw her parka in the backseat the next morning.

The next morning, Duane left for work at 8:30 am. As soon as he was gone, Loretta made sandwiches, packed the food, and packed a suitcase. After loading the food and suitcase into the car, she found her parka in the basement closet. She threw it into the back seat, along with a blue, wool blanket. Then she tidied the house and left a note on the kitchen table.

Duane: I'm taking my car and going away for a few days. No longer than a week. I have to figure things out. I've left you some sandwiches and fruit in the fridge. Don't worry about me.
Loretta

It was a windy morning, but mostly clear. Loretta was just about to pull out of the driveway when she remembered something. She had arranged for one of her customers to come by on Thursday to pick up the slacks she'd shortened. She'd have to drop them off on the way. She went back into the house and retrieved the slacks and the woman's address. It was going to take a while. The woman lived out in Fort Garry, in the south end of the city.

By the time Loretta turned on to the Trans-Canada highway, heading west, it was past 10:30.

When Duane got home from work and read the note, the first thing he did was call Loretta. Her phone went straight to voicemail. He folded the note and put it in his shirt pocket. Thinking Loretta may have gone to stay with a friend, he threw on his jacket and went back out to his truck. There were two places he thought Loretta might have gone: either to her friend Bev's or to Norm Jones' house, as she was friends with Norm's wife Rae. He drove over to the Jones house first, less than two miles away. There was no sign of Loretta's SUV. Then he drove over to Bev's house in St. Boniface. There was no one there and no sign of Loretta's car there, either. Duane was frustrated and angry, but he was also starting to feel a bit panicky and scared. He sat in his truck in front of Bev's house for an hour, waiting. No one came or went. The house remained dark. He took Loretta's note out of his pocket and read it again. Then he ripped it up and threw it out the window.

One month later, Duane Selby would face charges in connection with the disappearance of his wife, Loretta.

13 Heading West

October 18

Anyone who's driven across the prairies from Winnipeg to the mountains would say the same thing. Especially in the late fall. It's an exercise in outright monotony. Perhaps requiring a measure of latent masochism. Miles and miles of numbing highway, barren landscapes, and dull, endless skies. Between the dreary little towns and the vast empty spaces, it seems like all that's left standing are occasional stands of stubborn spruce trees.

Loretta had made the drive many times over her lifetime; in her childhood with her family, as a young woman with her sister and with friends, and a few times with Duane. So she wasn't in the least fazed by the prospect. As always, she was fortified by a deep cache of music: Tom Petty, The Traveling Wilburys, The Eagles, Neil Young, Clapton, Sting... She could turn up the volume as loud as she wanted. And there was no one to tell her to change the CD.

For the first part of the trip, Loretta listened to *Full Moon Fever*, one of her all-time favourite albums. She thought she'd stop in Moosomin for gas and coffee. There'd be a Tim's there. Then grab a burger in Regina and push on to Swift Current. She should make it by 8pm.

She thought about Jimmy. How could she have been such a fool? The deep shame she felt was starting to back off a little. *She* should have dumped *him* - a long time ago. Married men are all the same - that's what everyone said. They want to have their cake and eat it too. A devoted little wife at home and some nice pussy on the side. That's exactly who Jimmy was.

160

A number of times the day before, she'd been on the verge of calling him up, or calling his wife. Late on Monday night, she'd driven over to his house and parked on the street in front, and just sat there. She hoped he'd seen her. She'd been so close to getting out of the car and banging on his door. But she hadn't. Then she drove home.

It was good driving weather; the skies were mostly clear right into Saskatchewan. As the white SUV ate up the miles, Loretta's spite for Jimmy played out theatrically in her head. Jimmy didn't deserve to just slip back into his comfortable little world, she thought, with his adorable young daughters and his devoted wife. Maybe she should scare him a little. Give him a reality check. Have a little fun. She could send him a text, maybe something like "Hi Jimmy. Is everything back to normal? I sure hope so. I guess you're ready for visitors now?" Or she could trick him into meeting her, and then dump a bottle of perfume all over him. She'd seen that in a movie. Let him explain *that* to his wife. Maybe she'd leave the empty perfume bottle in his mailbox a few days later.

Such vengeful thoughts quickly gave way to a thick dose of conscience, creased with humiliation. Jimmy was a jerk, but it was her own doing. She wanted him. She fell in love him. She pressured him. He didn't want to be with her.

She thought about Duane. How was he going to react when he found the note? She just couldn't imagine him going crazy about it. He would probably just give it some time. Wait for a while to see how things went.

As Loretta's thoughts wandered, from Jimmy to Duane to Cathy, from the past to the future, she had to fight off a strong wave of guilt. She thought she didn't deserve to feel that way, but she still did. Guilt about leaving Duane. But why should she have to keep living the same dismal life? She deserved to be happy, to do things she wanted to do.

161

Didn't everyone deserve that? And anyway, Duane would be all right. He'd just have to learn to cook for himself. He probably wouldn't miss her a whole lot. He hardly ever paid any attention to what she was doing or what she was thinking.

Still, Duane was a good man in his own way, Loretta thought, slipping *Hotel California* into the CD player, a half-hour from Regina. He'd always treated her fairly, respectfully, paid his share. He worked hard. He never asked anybody for anything. It was funny, she thought, the image people had of Duane. People thought he was such a scary, volatile guy - that he was likely to lose his temper over absolutely nothing and turn violent. He *did* have a temper. She'd seen it many times, especially in his younger days. But it was almost always because people pushed him too far; they did something that really pissed him off. You certainly didn't want to pick a fight with him. But even in their younger days, Duane's hot temper and surly disposition had never frightened her or turned her off, like it had other people. He had never once directed it at her. It had actually made her feel safe; protected. That was one of the things that had attracted her to him when they first went out. He made her feel safe. No one was ever going to threaten her or take advantage of her.

He'd respected her pretty well, she thought. But it just wasn't enough.

Approaching Regina, Loretta switched from her CD's to a local AM radio station. The news was on. O.J. Simpson was out of jail. Slow news day, Loretta thought. The rest of the news was split. There were the latest celebrities taken down by sexual harassment charges and then more pointless bullshit about Donald Trump.

By the time Loretta pulled into the Husky truck stop in Regina, it was after four o'clock. It felt good to have put so

162

many miles behind her. She looked in the mirror, running the tips of her fingers across her face. Reasonably satisfied, she grabbed her green leather jacket and her handbag and got out of the car. It felt cold, a lot colder than when she'd left Winnipeg. She would fill up the tank and then have a hamburger and fries, she thought. She hadn't had a hamburger in months.

As she filled the tank, she looked out on the highway. She was starting to feel tired. Moose Jaw was an hour away. Swift Current was another two hours after Moose Jaw. Maybe she'd stop in Moose Jaw for the night. There was no point pushing it. Five hours to Calgary the next day or seven hours, it didn't make much difference.

The restaurant looked like countless other diners and truck-stops: shiny, wood-edged arborite tables and matching chairs; ketchup, sugar, salt, pepper, and a rack of assorted jams on each table; low grey walls dividing the room into sections; friendly, uniformed servers, refilling everyone's coffee again and again. Loretta took a seat at a table for two. Within seconds, a pleasant woman with a pile of streaked hair took Loretta's order: a cheeseburger and fries and a glass of water.

Loretta looked around. It was mostly individual men seated at the tables, Caucasians in their forties, some in pairs, except for the table right across from hers, where a young couple had just been served their dinners. Loretta smiled as she glanced over at them. They looked very young, in their early twenties. The young man was lanky and blonde-haired, wearing a plaid shirt. He had a scruffy beard and a prominent tattoo on his neck. Across from him was a pretty young woman with fluorescent red hair, wearing bright red lipstick and pale make-up. She had piercings in her ears, her nose and her bottom lip. What really caught Loretta's eye was the guitar case. It had been placed protectively, upright, between the inside seat and the wall, to the right of the blonde-haired man. They made a great couple, Loretta thought. Probably crazy in love, making big plans, facing the world together. She strained to catch a bit of their conversation, but they were intent on their food and said little.

Loretta wolfed down her cheeseburger. The rest of the trip, she'd eat healthy, she vowed; she'd stick to the food she'd brought. The young couple left a few minutes before she did, guitar in tow. Loretta laughed ironically to herself; even here she couldn't get away from guitar players.

Back in her SUV, Loretta thought again about how much farther she wanted to drive that day. It was four-forty. Moose Jaw was about an hour away. She'd see if she felt like going farther when she got there.

When Loretta pulled onto the highway, she saw them immediately, the young couple from the restaurant. They were a hundred feet or so along the highway, hitchhiking, holding up a paper sign: *Moose Jaw*. Of course, Loretta thought. They'd probably caught a ride to the Husky with a trucker. She didn't hesitate to pull over and pick them up. As she did, she grabbed her small handbag from the passenger seat and placed it on the floor, at her feet. Not that a couple hitchhiking together was anything to fear. She liked the look of them, especially the fact that the man was toting a guitar. And she could use a little company.

The two jumped into the car, introducing themselves as Robbie and Jaylynn. Robbie got into the front seat, laying his backpack on the floor. Jaylynn took the backseat behind Loretta, along with the guitar, following Loretta's directions to throw the cooler and the blanket into the cargo area.

Within minutes, Loretta was treated to a flood of details about the couple, with Robbie doing almost all the talking. They were both 21, he told Loretta, and they'd both grown up nearby, in rural Saskatchewan. Robbie was from a small farming community outside Chamberlain, thirty-five miles

164

north of Moose Jaw. Jaylynn was from the small town of Bethune, forty miles northwest of Regina on Highway 11. They'd met in high school, in Moose Jaw. They'd spent the past month in Toronto, trying to get enough gigs to live on. They did folk songs and country songs. Jaylynn sang all the lead vocals. It hadn't gone so well, and after running through all their money, they were returning home for a while. They'd hitchhiked all the way, spending a few nights in bus stations along the way, bumming money from whoever they could. There were lots of good people in the world, Robbie said to Loretta, people like her, people that were glad to help them out. They'd be grateful if Loretta would drop them off at Moose Jaw, near the turn-off to Highway 2.

Loretta told them she'd been around bands all her life - her husband was a guitar player. His band played sixties rock and roll. They were called *The Drones*. She was heading to her sister's place in Canmore.

Their parents had been totally against their going to Toronto, Robbie told Loretta; they should have been either going to college or finding a job. I guess you're only young once, Loretta commented, trying to sound sympathetic.

In a short forty-five minutes they were coming up on Moose Jaw. The sun was starting to set. Loretta was thinking she'd call it quits for the day; find a motel somewhere along the highway in Moose Jaw.

Robbie turned to Jaylynn in the back seat. 'I guess we'll get out just before the junction' he said to her.

'Where should I drop you?' Loretta asked Robbie.

'There's an access road just before Number 2. We're almost there. There's room to pull off the highway there. We'll jump out and you can keep going. Here it is, right here.'

As directed, Loretta pulled off the highway onto the wide shoulder where the access road began. If she'd looked more

165

closely, she would have thought it was an odd place for the young couple to get out. The access road was nothing but a dirt road that ran about a mile parallel to the highway, linking up with number 2. Why wouldn't they have just got out at 2? But there was no reason to size the situation up any more carefully.

Loretta put the car in park and undid her seat belt, intending to shake hands with Jaylynn and wish the couple a cheerful "good luck". To her complete surprise, Robbie, having undone his seat belt, reached across and turned the key off in the ignition, and then removed it, putting it into his pants pocket. 'What are you doing?' Loretta said to him, realizing simultaneously what was happening.

Robbie reached over with his right hand and grasped Loretta's right forearm firmly. Loretta recoiled, shifting her weight against the car door. 'We aren't going to hurt you' said Robbie. 'We just want money. Okay?' He released Loretta's arm and reached for his backpack on the floor. To Loretta's horror, he pulled out a long hunting knife, which he held up for her to see. 'Now, we're going take a little ride to an ATM, okay? You're going to withdraw some cash and then we'll drop you off somewhere, safe and sound, okay? I don't need to hurt you.'

Robbie kept his eyes on Loretta but spoke to Jaylynn. 'I think her purse must be in the back there. It's not up here. Check her purse, Jaylynn.'

Loretta was still wearing her leather jacket. Most of her cash, some twelve hundred dollars, was neatly tucked away in the inside pocket. She made a quick calculation. To run. She'd run along the highway and flag down a car. Traffic wasn't that heavy, but cars were going by every minute or so. If they chased her, hopefully someone would see them and stop and help her. If not, she'd just run; keep running; take her chances. Maybe they'd just take the cash in her purse and drive off with the car. They had the keys.

166

'It's here' said Loretta. 'It's right here, on the floor.' She reached down with her right hand and caught hold of the small handbag, and then handed it to Robbie.

As Robbie began to look through the handbag, Loretta made her move. She quickly reached for the door handle with her left hand and pushed the door open. Before Robbie could move to stop her, she was almost out of the car. 'Jaylynn!' he cried out. 'Get out and grab her! She's getting out.'

Jaylynn reacted as fast as she could, but by the time she was out of the car, Loretta was clear of the door and running along the shoulder of the highway, waving her right hand in the air. One car and then another drove right by. Meanwhile, Robbie had also gotten out of the car and began to chase after Loretta, still brandishing the hunting knife. 'We can't let her go' he yelled to Jaylynn. Uncertain what to do, Jaylynn remained near the car.

Deliberately or not, Loretta was running with the traffic, on the right side of the road. Running for her life. She could see lights up ahead, a mile or so up the highway, at the junction of the Trans-Canada with Highway 2. Robbie ran after her as fast as he could. Loretta's speed was no match for his. She began to gasp and falter after sprinting a few hundred meters. Still desperately waving her right hand in the air, she knew she wasn't going to outrun Robbie. She stopped cold, and bent over forward, trying to catch her breath. At the same moment, Robbie caught up to her and lunged at her, stabbing her in the back. Because of Loretta's stooped, stationary position and Robbie's speed, the long blade of the hunting knife penetrated deeply into Loretta's back. She cried out, a horrible, helpless cry, and fell to the ground, bleeding heavily. Another car zoomed by. Robbie looked back along the highway. He could see another set of headlights approaching in the dusk. He looked at Loretta. He hadn't intended to stab her like that. He'd lost control.

She was obviously very badly wounded. She was hardly even moving.

The young man pulled Loretta further away from the highway, off the shoulder. He left her lying there and ran back to the car, where his partner had remained standing during the short chase. 'What happened?' she said, terrified, when he reached the SUV. 'What the fuck happened? What did you do?'

'Get in the car. Get in the car. I stabbed her, okay? I didn't mean to stab her like that. She stopped and I - We have to get out of here.'

'We can't just leave her there. What's the matter with you, Cameron? We have to take her to a hospital or something. Fuck. How badly is she hurt?'

The young man, whose real name was Cameron, got into the car, behind the wheel. The young woman, whose real name was Sarah, walked around to the other side of the car and got in the passenger side.

'I don't know' said Cameron, highly agitated, taking the car keys out of his pocket. 'Pretty bad. She's really bleeding. We can't take her to a hospital. We'll go to jail.'

'Maybe we can just drop her off somewhere' said Sarah. 'Close to a hospital, and then leave. Call up an ambulance to pick her up. We can be gone before they get there.'

'I don't know' said Cameron. 'I think we should just leave. Right now. We can head back to Regina. We can dump the car there and figure out what to do.'

Sarah opened the door on her side and got out of the SUV. 'I'm not going unless we get her some help. I'm not. You can go if you want to.'

'Okay, okay' said Cameron, with panic in his voice. 'Okay. Let's get her into the back seat. I'll drive the car up to her.'

Sarah got back in and they pulled the car up alongside Loretta. Cameron turned off the ignition and they got out.

Loretta wasn't moving and had obviously lost a lot of blood.

'Oh my god, Cameron. What the fuck!'

'Do you want to get her in the car or what?'

'Look how much she's bleeding. She's not moving, Cameron.'

'Grab that blanket that's in the back of the car. We'll wrap it around her.'

Sarah got the blanket. They wrapped it around Loretta and the two of them dragged her up off the shoulder of the highway and into the back seat of the SUV. A car sped past. They got back into the car.

Sarah was nearly hysterical. 'She's not moving, Cameron. She's not moving. Is she dead? Did you fucking kill her? Is she dead?'

'I don't know' said Cameron. 'I don't know. I didn't mean to stab her like that. What are we going to do? What the fuck are we going to do? I don't want to go to jail for the rest of my life.' He started the car up.

Things hadn't gone according to plan. The young couple were a pair of small-time thieves, both 20 years of age. The story they'd fed Loretta was entirely bogus, made up and rehearsed. Both were originally from Saskatoon. They'd both left home right after high school. They had been in Regina for the past summer and early fall, breaking into cars and houses to score cash. The only part of their story that was semi-truthful was the music part. Cameron really did play the guitar - though not particularly well - and he and Sarah did play songs together. But they only ever played for friends and they knew only a handful of songs. They'd never played a single gig.

If the story Cameron told Loretta had sounded authentic, it was because Cameron really did have a strong connection with Moose Jaw. His dad's sister and her kids lived in

Moose Jaw. Cameron had spent three full summers there in his high school years, staying with his cousins. He knew the area and the nearby towns well.

While in Regina, the two nervy young thieves had formulated a straightforward plan. They wanted to head out to Vancouver Island, to Victoria. They would hitchhike, and score some cash from the first likely source - an elderly couple or a trusting woman who was travelling by herself. They would take over the car and have her withdraw as much money as she could from an ATM. Then they'd drop her off somewhere remote, maybe on the outskirts of a city like Calgary. They'd ditch the car and buy tickets for a Greyhound going west.

When they'd set off from the Husky station in Regina, the two young travellers had no idea how fast the perfect opportunity was going to drop into their laps. They had practised their parts, gone over the story they were going to tell. Cameron would signal Sarah when he thought the time was right to make a move. He would do the talking. She just had to follow directions; play the supporting role. The knife was only intended to scare the potential mark. They had always carried it for their own protection.

Cameron and Sarah sat in the car for a moment, with their hearts pounding, on the shoulder of the highway, with the motor running and the headlights off.

'What if she's dead?' said Sarah, looking with dread at the motionless figure in the back seat. 'She hasn't moved, Cameron. I think she's dead. My god.'

'Are you sure?' said Cameron, looking back at Loretta himself. 'Are you sure she hasn't moved?'

'Yes' said Sarah. 'Look at her. She's not moving.'

'Okay, okay. I have to think. Let me think. Okay... Listen, Sarah. Okay? We have to both calm down. We have to get rid of the car and her and everything. If we took the car and

170

left her somewhere, they'd be looking for us in no time. Plus, if we got stopped, I don't even have an up-to-date licence, remember? And the back seat is probably covered in blood.'

'What are we going to do, Cameron? I'm scared. I don't know what we should do.'

'I know. I know. Let's think, okay? How much money is in her purse? Could you check it? Please? Or hand it to me. It's on the floor.'

Sarah passed the small handbag over to Cameron.

'We'll get out of this' said Cameron, counting the money. 'I promise. I've got an idea, okay?' There was a hundred and eighty dollars.

'What are we going to do?'

'See where we are? We're a mile from Highway 2, right? That's the junction right up there. See? We can turn onto 2. We can drive the car up there and leave it in the bush, off the main road. There's lots of dirt roads off 2 that go nowhere, into the bush. We'll just have to walk back a few miles. Then we can hitchhike into town from the junction. Take a bus out of Moose Jaw in the morning. Or maybe we shouldn't stay here. We can hitchhike back to Regina and wait there until morning. We'll be gone before anybody knows anything. I know a couple of roads off 2. We used to go drinking out there in the summer. When I was in high school. Me and my cousin. Okay? Let's give it a shot. Okay? Let's get going. It's almost dark.'

Cameron turned the headlights on and pulled out. After turning north on Highway 2, Cameron drove past the first turn-off and then the second. He took the third road off 2, Garland Road, turning east. It was a dirt road, in fairly rough shape.

The truth of the matter was that Cameron didn't know these side roads at all. As he'd told Sarah, he *had* gone drinking off highway 2 a few times, with his cousin, but his

171

memory was vague. His cousin had always done the driving. After following Garland Road into the bush for a short way, bumping along, they came to a barrier, consisting of two heavy iron arms chained together in the middle. The barrier ran from one side of the road to the other. There was a rusty metal sign hanging from one of the arms: *No Entrance Road Closed* To Cameron, as scared as he was, the thought of turning around didn't even register. He drove off the road, around the barrier, into the brush, glancing off a tree as he brought the SUV back onto the road. They followed the uneven, rocky road for another mile or so, up a small hill, eventually coming to a clearing, where they saw two old, rundown buildings, about thirty feet apart. Cameron pulled the SUV off the road and in between the two buildings.

'Okay, let's leave it here' Cameron said to Sarah. He turned off the ignition and switched off the headlights. It was almost completely dark. He took the keys out of the ignition and put them in his pocket. 'Let's get out of here' he said. 'We've got a long walk back to the junction. We should put on our sweaters. It's cold.'

As they were about to leave, Cameron pocketed Loretta's iPhone from her handbag.

'Why are you taking her phone?' Sarah asked.

'They can track her. We can throw it away later somewhere. Maybe in Regina. It could buy us some time. I'll turn it off.'

The two young lovers, scared but still united, made their way back down the dirt road. In the darkness sat the white SUV, with Loretta Selby's lifeless body extended across the back seat.

14 MPC

October 25 - January 12

In a matter of twelve short days, Loretta Selby's road trip to the mountains was wholly transformed; from an emotional escape to a missing person case. Such cases were an increasingly sensitive and visible part of police work in Canada. The ongoing National Inquiry into Missing and Murdered Indigenous Women had focused public scrutiny on all aspects of the police response to reports of missing women. It may be debatable as to the role this played in the investigation of Loretta Selby's disappearance. But it must be noted that the response was both quick and comprehensive. No resources were spared, especially by the Winnipeg Police.

On Wednesday, October 25, one week after Loretta had left the note, Duane Selby called his sister-in-law Cathy Barr-Middleton in Calgary. In Loretta's note, she had said she wouldn't be gone for more than a week. Duane had been calling her cellphone intermittently over the past three days, with no response.

Remembering her conversation with Loretta, Cathy knew that Loretta may have left Winnipeg as late as October 21 or October 22. She also kept her word and didn't disclose Loretta's destination to Duane.

Relations between Cathy and Duane were considerably less strained than between Bob and Duane. Still, their conversations were polite at best and invariably quite short.

173

'Hi Cathy. It's Duane.'

'Hi Duane. How's it going?'

'Not bad. Listen, I'm wondering if you've heard from Loretta.'

'Excuse me?'

'Have you heard from Loretta? Things haven't been going so great between us lately. She told me she was getting away for a few days. I haven't heard from her. She doesn't answer her cellphone.'

'Sorry, I haven't.'

'Do you know where she is, Cathy?'

'No, I don't. Sorry, Duane.'

'Is she out there with you?'

'Duane, I have no idea where she is, okay? She'll probably contact you.'

'Okay. Thanks.'

On Sunday evening, October 29, Cathy called Duane. The anticipated period for Loretta's stay in the condo had come and gone. Cathy had left voice messages for the building manager for the past three days, to call back as soon as he had a chance. Had her sister Loretta arrived? Had she left already? Gary, the building manager, was a dedicated hiker. At that time, almost all of the units in his building were unoccupied. So he was spending most days on the trails, both in Canmore and in Banff. As a result, he and Cathy played telephone tag for three days. Cathy didn't learn until Sunday that Loretta had made no appearance at all at the condo. Very alarmed, she called Duane.

'Hi, Duane. It's Cathy. I'm worried about Loretta. Have you heard from her?'

'No. Nothing. I've been calling her and texting her, but there's no answer.'

'She was supposed to be coming out here. To the condo in Kananaskis. She called me more than a week ago and told me about her plans. She asked me not to say anything to you. But she never showed up. She hasn't called me either. She should have called me by now. I'm worried about her.'

That night, and again the next morning, Duane spoke to a number of individuals at the District 2 office of the Winnipeg Police Department. He was interviewed in his home after work on Monday, October 30, by a detective named Bonnie Henderson, where he disclosed everything he knew about the situation. Loretta had left him a note, he told the detective, but he'd thrown it away. She had told him she needed to get away for a while, that she wasn't happy. As far as he was concerned, things between them were much as they always had been. Was there anyone she might have been involved with, the detective asked, putting it delicately. Duane's answer was not that he knew of.

On Tuesday, October 31, Moose Jaw recorded its first heavy snowfall of the season, blanketing the city and the surrounding countryside. It promised to be an especially cold winter, so the snow was quite possibly there to stay. On the same day, a representative of the Winnipeg Police interviewed Cathy Barr-Middleton, Loretta's sister, by telephone. She conveyed a lot of information that Duane hadn't, chiefly that Loretta was planning to leave the marriage and that she had had an affair with a guitar player named Ian Cooper. Cathy stated that, though she wasn't sure, she had the feeling that the affair was still going on when she last spoke to Loretta. Loretta had said nothing about it during that conversation. Cathy also said she didn't think Duane knew about Ian Cooper, though she didn't know that for a fact.

By the end of the week, the same Ian Cooper had been located and interviewed by police. He was living with his girlfriend, the same woman he'd been with, on and off, during the time he was involved with Loretta. Cooper freely admitted to the affair, telling police that it had ended some two years ago. He'd had no contact of any kind with Loretta since they'd broken off.

A nation-wide alert was issued for Loretta's vehicle, the white SUV, on November 1. Canadian border officials were also engaged in the search. By November 7, no trace of the vehicle had yet been reported. On that date, a police spokesperson appeared on television, describing Loretta's disappearance and appealing for information.

On Thursday, November 9, in the late afternoon, Jimmy Green walked into the Winnipeg Police headquarters on Smith Street and offered a detailed statement to officials. Jimmy and his wife Karen had discussed the matter at length the night before, following the televised announcement of Loretta's disappearance on November 7. Jimmy, now firmly committed to a program of total honesty, didn't have to think twice about submitting his account. Karen was concerned about what their daughters would learn and how the publicity would affect all of their lives. Jimmy promised to ask the police to treat discreetly the information he would give. There would hopefully be no need to publicize his name. Both Jimmy and Karen were convinced, incorrectly, that Duane knew about the affair. They both thought it was only a matter of time until Jimmy was drawn into the case anyway.

Jimmy's statement to police was comprehensive and unflinching. All of the history and details of his meetings with Loretta Selby were clearly and accurately recounted. Even the name Johnny La Montina found its way into the police file.

176

Greg Mazur had also seen the announcement of Loretta's disappearance. He was in possession of crucial information regarding the matter, he believed. Loretta had been having an affair. He'd witnessed it with his own eyes. He even remembered the type of vehicle the guy drove, as well as its licence plate: ROCKON. In Greg's mind, there could only be one explanation for Loretta's disappearance: Duane had found out about the affair and killed her. If the police were informed about the affair, it would logically point them in the right direction. Greg's hostility for Duane had never gone away, and now he was going to find it immensely satisfying to tip off the cops.

Greg's vengeful enthusiasm had a curious consequence. It was highly likely, he thought, that he would be called to testify at what would surely be a major trial. It was the kind of spectacular case that would be covered by all local and national media. As a result, one minor detail in his account would require creative adjustment: the location where he'd seen Loretta and the guy that night. His girlfriend Ricki would be following the case closely, like everyone else. If Ricki learned he'd been right outside Johnny La Montina's place, she would know he'd been spying on her. So he would change the location slightly, from the bay off Lanark to a nearby stretch of Academy Road. It wouldn't matter, anyway.

On the morning of Friday, November 10, Greg Mazur phoned in his tip to the police. It was the day after Jimmy Green had been interviewed. Greg's call was patched through to the lead investigator in the case, Detective Bonnie Henderson, to whom he provided his personal details. The detective was impressed by such a willing witness, the second in as many days. Greg described his connection to Duane and Loretta, through The Drones. He characterized Duane as a very aggressive guy with a

177

bullying streak and an explosive temper. A guy who could lose it over almost nothing. Greg also told the detective about the hostile, near-violent confrontation that had marked his final day in the band.

Greg went on to describe what he had seen on the night of October 9. He was in his cab, he said, parked on the south side of Academy Road, adjacent to the Starbucks parking lot. He was taking a short break, sipping a cup of coffee he'd purchased. It was 7pm, give or take a few minutes, he recalled. A Jeep Wrangler pulled up and parked right in front of him. He couldn't help but remember the licence plate: ROCKON. The man driving the jeep got out and walked over to the sidewalk. A few minutes later, a white SUV pulled up, and stopped on the street, right beside the jeep. The man walked over and jumped into the SUV. When the man opened the door, Greg got a good look at the woman behind the wheel. It was Loretta Selby. Loretta and the man kissed romantically and then the SUV drove off. Greg told the detective that he also recognized the SUV - a Hyundai - from his days in the band.

After clarifying a few details, Detective Henderson thanked Greg for the call. She asked him if he could come down to the station in the near future and sign the written record of their conversation, to which he agreed.

A quick licence plate search identified Jimmy Green as the owner of the jeep Greg had observed. As far as the police were concerned, Greg's testimony simply corroborated Jimmy Green's own statement.

Within the first week of the police investigation, Duane Selby became an obvious suspect. Following Jimmy Green's interview, a warrant was obtained to search Duane's house. Duane was entirely co-operative, leaving the house unlocked as he left for work on Monday, November 13. When he returned from work that day, the forensics team was still in the house, getting ready to finish up for the day. At that time, Duane also accommodated the team's request to search and examine his truck and another vehicle inside the garage.

Evidence uncovered was scant, but decisive. Nothing of interest was found on either of the two laptops in the Selby house. A comprehensive search of the house - drawers, closets, cabinets, clothes, guitar cases, ceiling tiles and the like - yielded no relevant physical evidence. But a sweep of the floors, tables and other surfaces in the house revealed something very compelling. There were minute traces of blood on the kitchen floor, in the main upstairs hallway, and on the mat in the bathroom. With 36 hours, a DNA comparison with hair from a hairbrush of Loretta's confirmed the blood to be hers. The police returned to the Selby house and swept Duane's Ford truck. Traces of Loretta's blood were also found on the floor carpeting in the back seat of the truck.

Though the police could not possibly have known, the minimal traces of blood they found were the result of a totally irrelevant sequence of events. Just prior to her departure, Loretta had cut her finger and drawn blood in slicing a pineapple. She had bandaged the small cut in the bathroom and cleaned up the small amount of blood there and in the kitchen. When she went looking for a windshield scraper in Duane's truck, specks of blood were transferred to the floor carpeting in the back seat.

On Friday, November 17, police charged and arrested Duane Selby in connection with Loretta's disappearance. The initial charges were kidnapping and forcible confinement. Duane was taken into custody, from where he contacted his brother to find him a lawyer. Three days later, he was granted interim release, using the equity in his house to post bail and agreeing to remain in the city and appear in court when called.

On Friday, December 1, a little after 5:30pm, a police detective named Arnold Horn paid Greg Mazur a short visit. Horn was a junior detective, working under Bonnie Henderson. Greg had readily agreed to the meeting, intended to clarify a few details in his statement, as the detective had said. The meeting took place at Ricki Clark's side-by-side in Southdale, where Greg was living. Ricki was also present at that time, having returned from work an hour earlier.

Horn was a keen and ambitious young detective, and had carefully poured over the details of all the evidence in the Loretta Selby case. He had discovered a small discrepancy. Jimmy Green's statement placed his vehicle in front of Johnny La Montina's house on October 9, where he said Loretta had picked him up, from 6:45pm to almost 10pm. Greg Mazur had said he saw Loretta pick Jimmy up on Academy Road.

It was a very short meeting. Arnold Horn sat across the living room from Ricki and Greg, who were sitting side-by-side on the sofa. 'Mr. Mazur' began the detective. 'You said that you saw Loretta Selby, in a white Hyundai SUV, pick up a man on Academy Road around 7pm on October 9. The man who had parked his jeep, correct?'

'That's right' said Greg.

'Good. Okay. Just confirming. We have other evidence that Loretta Selby picked up the same man, on the same day, at that same time, but on Lanark Street, around 103 Lanark Street. I'm just trying to clarify. Are you absolutely sure about the time and location?'

Greg was taken off-guard. 'Um, yah' he said. 'I'm sure.'

'Okay. Thanks very much. I appreciate your time. Good night. Good night, Ms. Clark.'

Greg's police interview didn't immediately ring a bell for Ricki Clark. But it did a few minutes later, when she was in the kitchen preparing dinner, remembering as she did the address of her guitar teacher, Johnny La Montina. 101 Lanark. She flew out of the kitchen and confronted Greg.

'What were you doing at 103 Lanark at 7 o'clock on a Monday, Greg? You were spying on me, weren't you?'

On Tuesday, December 26, Loretta Selby's body was discovered, in her white SUV, by two cross-country skiers in Moose Jaw, Saskatchewan. The vehicle was parked at the end of Garland Road, where it was mostly covered by snow. Moose Jaw police, with the assistance of the local RCMP detachment, readily determined the cause of death and produced an accurate estimate for the time of death.

On Friday, January 12, 2018, all charges against Duane Selby were dropped. The Winnipeg Police Department issued a short statement to the media: Loretta Selby's body had been found and a murder investigation was under way. Duane Selby was no longer a suspect in the case.

15 Echoes

For anyone close to Loretta Selby or her husband Duane, for anyone who had ever played in The Drones, for anyone directly connected to the circumstances of Loretta's death, life would never be the same. Though fate was hardly even-handed.

If getting away with murder can be called good luck, then Cameron and Sarah, the two young travellers in Saskatchewan, received a more-than-generous share. It was simply a matter of blind chance that Garland Road, where they had left the white SUV, was so well-suited to their purposes. The property at the end of Garland Road was in fact the site of a former diesel-fuel station. It had served the agricultural community in the area until the late nineteen nineties. Better options became available in the area and the business and property were abandoned. When the owner moved to sell the property, the municipality ordered him to clean up the toxic effects of the diesel fuel over the years. Facing enormous costs, the owner simply walked away and the land was condemned. Garland Road and the property were blocked off. Before October 18, it had been more than two years since any vehicle had found its way up the fateful road.

Fortune smiled on the two young itinerants in a second way, in the timely arrival of snow. With a heavy snowfall at the end of October, and an early winter setting in, the SUV was largely hidden from view, even from the east.

After leaving Garland Road, Cameron and Sarah had soon after hitched a ride back to Regina, where Loretta's phone was deposited in a dumpster. The phone was never recovered. The next day, the cash from Loretta's handbag was used to purchase two bus tickets to Calgary. As soon as they raised enough money to get to Vancouver, they left Calgary. They eventually made their way to Tofino, where both found jobs in the same restaurant-bar. As for their roles in the death of Loretta Selby, no suspicion was ever likely to fall their way. As long as they kept their secret.

On Saturday, December 2, the day after Greg Mazur's embarrassing interview with Detective Arnold Horn, Ricki Clark kicked Greg out. She had finally had enough of his obsessive jealousy. After Greg left for work in the evening, she had the locks changed. She texted him, promising that his belongings would be delivered to his apartment on Monday. Greg didn't take the decision lightly and created an ugly scene later that night.

As Greg was a member of Ricki's band, she really only had one option. She informed the others that she was quitting the band. In the following days, she decided to form her own band and posted notices online seeking applicants.

Over the next few months, Greg was relentless in trying to meet with Ricki. She wanted nothing more to do with him. When he persisted in coming around her home, she obtained a restraining order against him.

For the time being, Karen and Jimmy Green remained together, while continuing to sleep apart. As far as their children were concerned, Jimmy's snoring was the reason. Otherwise, for the most part, their home and work lives continued as usual. Karen remained emotionally distant, while Jimmy fervently hoped they could see their way through somehow. Toward the end of January, after hearing Jimmy mention counselling so many times, Karen called him on it. As a result, the couple embarked on marriage counselling, with Jimmy pinning his hopes on the redoubtable Dr. Sylvia Wennapulko.

In the wake of Loretta's death, Jimmy decided to permanently break from the local music scene. He felt genuine pain and deep remorse for his indirect role in Loretta's demise. He thought it might be good to talk to Duane one day, about everything. Or maybe not.

By January 12, when the police declared that Duane Selby was no longer a suspect, Duane was a broken man. He had bravely faced Loretta's rejection of him prior to her leaving. He had wrongly suffered the deep humiliation of being charged in her disappearance. He had been struck dumb by the news of her death and by the violent manner of her death.

From the beginning, with the exception of Norm and Rae Jones and Duane's brother Ralph, everyone believed Duane responsible for his wife's disappearance: friends, present and former bandmates, co-workers, neighbours, his sister-in-law Cathy, her husband Bob... Even his brother started to have his doubts as time went on.

Following the news that Loretta's body had been discovered, Duane decided to take some time off work. It would be a long time before he would regain his pride and his self-confidence; before other people regarded him with a reasonable level of trust and respect again. A long time to overcome his sorrow over the loss of Loretta.

Once Duane had been cleared of all charges, Cathy Barr-Middleton, Loretta's sister, called him to pass on some information. He was the beneficiary of Loretta's life insurance policy - the policy that had accompanied her pension investment. Duane would be receiving an amount of seventy-five thousand dollars from IP Investors in due course.

Duane would certainly be able to put the money to good use, especially because he would be off work for a number of weeks. He had legal expenses to pay and home expenses to deal with. When there was no sign of the insurance payment after a few months had passed, Duane began making inquiries. Even though he had been completely cleared of any wrong-doing in connection with Loretta's death, the insurance company put up a series of roadblocks. It would be more than a year before Duane saw the money. During that time, he called the company many times, only to be stonewalled. At one point during the process, the aftermath of Loretta's death and the prolonged stress finally got to Duane. Reacting to a particularly trying series of unreturned calls, he paid a visit in person to the Winnipeg office of IP Investors. He was met by a dismissive lawyer who did nothing but obfuscate and throw big words at him. It was then, for the only time since Loretta's death, that Duane lost his temper. He grabbed the lawyer by the shirt collar and landed a vicious punch, square to the man's face. The lawyer suffered severe contusions and a broken nose. Duane was charged with assault, to which he pleaded guilty. He issued an apology and paid a fine of five hundred dollars.

THE END

About The Author

John Ginsburg was born in the northern Canadian mining town of Flin Flon, Manitoba. He presently lives in Winnipeg.